CLAIRE'S CHOCOLATE MOUSSE

4 one-ounce squares of semisweet chocolate,
   cut into chunks
3 eggs, separated
1 tsp vanilla
¾ tsp cream of tartar
½ cup sugar
1½ cups chilled whipping cream, separated

Avoid the hotter issues with the man in your life
by heating the chocolate in a 2-quart saucepan
over low heat, stirring occasionally. When the
chocolate is melted, remove pan from heat. In a
separate bowl, beat egg yolks slightly, then stir
yolks and vanilla into chocolate.

In a separate bowl (make *him* wash the dishes!),
beat the egg whites and cream of tartar until
foamy. Beat in sugar, a tablespoon at a time.
Stir ¼ of the meringue into the chocolate mixture,
then gently fold the rest in.

Take out frustrations by beating 1 cup of whipping
cream in a chilled bowl until stiff. Fold into the
chocolate mixture. Divide evenly among bowls,
making sure you leave enough in mixing bowl to
taste the mousse—to ensure it's perfect, of course.

Beat remaining whipping cream, but don't get too
distracted by thoughts of a sexy dark-haired man
and end up overbeating it. Carefully drop dollops
on each bowl of mousse. Refrigerate at least two
hours before sharing with someone delectable.

Dear Reader,

Discover a guilt-free way to enjoy this holiday season. Treat yourself to four calorie-free, but oh-so-satisfying brand-new Silhouette Romance titles this month.

Start with *Santa Brought a Son* (#1698) by Melissa McClone. This heartwarming reunion romance is the fourth book in Silhouette Romance's new six-book continuity, MARRYING THE BOSS'S DAUGHTER.

Would a duty-bound prince forsake tradition to marry an enchanting commoner? Find out in *The Prince & the Marriage Pact* (#1699), the latest episode in THE CARRAMER TRUST miniseries by reader favorite Valerie Parv.

Then, it's anyone's guess if a wacky survival challenge can end happily ever after. Join the fun as the romantic winners of a crazy contest are revealed in *The Bachelor's Dare* (#1700) by Shirley Jump.

And in Donna Clayton's *The Nanny's Plan* (#1701), a would-be sophisticate is put through the ringer by a drop-dead gorgeous, absentminded professor and his rascally twin nephews.

So pick a cozy spot, relax and enjoy all four of these tender holiday confections that Silhouette Romance has cooked up just for you.

Happy holidays!

Mavis C. Allen
Associate Senior Editor

Please address questions and book requests to:
Silhouette Reader Service
U.S.: 3010 Walden Ave., P.O. Box 1325, Buffalo, NY 14269
Canadian: P.O. Box 609, Fort Erie, Ont. L2A 5X3

The Bachelor's Dare

SHIRLEY JUMP

SILHOUETTE *Romance*®

Published by Silhouette Books

America's Publisher of Contemporary Romance

To Jeff, and the memories of all those
long car rides between Massachusetts and Indiana.
I fell in love with you sometime between
the first toll booth and the last exit.

SILHOUETTE BOOKS

ISBN 0-373-19700-4

THE BACHELOR'S DARE

Copyright © 2003 by Shirley Kawa-Jump

All rights reserved. Except for use in any review, the reproduction
or utilization of this work in whole or in part in any form by any
electronic, mechanical or other means, now known or hereafter
invented, including xerography, photocopying and recording, or in
any information storage or retrieval system, is forbidden without
the written permission of the editorial office, Silhouette Books,
233 Broadway, New York, NY 10279 U.S.A.

All characters in this book have no existence outside the imagination of
the author and have no relation whatsoever to anyone bearing the same
name or names. They are not even distantly inspired by any individual
known or unknown to the author, and all incidents are pure invention.

This edition published by arrangement with Harlequin Books S.A.

® and TM are trademarks of Harlequin Books S.A., used under license.
Trademarks indicated with ® are registered in the United States Patent
and Trademark Office, the Canadian Trade Marks Office and in other
countries.

Visit Silhouette at www.eHarlequin.com

Printed in U.S.A.

Books by Shirley Jump

Silhouette Romance

The Virgin's Proposal #1641
The Bachelor's Dare #1700

SHIRLEY JUMP

has been a writer ever since she learned to read. She sold her first article at the age of eleven and from there, became a reporter and finally a freelance writer. However, she always maintained the dream of writing fiction, too. Since then, she has made a full-time career out of writing, dividing her time between articles, non-fiction books and romance. With a husband, two children and a houseful of pets, inspiration abounds in her life, giving her good fodder for writing and a daily workout for her sense of humor.

SURVIVE AND DRIVE CONTESTANTS

* Mark Dole: confirmed bachelor, used to work with his brother, Luke, in a software design company in California, but has never forgotten the girl next door, Claire

* Claire Richards: former hairdresser, knows Mark from childhood and doesn't intend to play fair in the contest—or in love

* Millie and Lester: a retired couple given to power shakes and napping, determined to win the RV, even if they have to resort to threats with knitting needles

* Danny: football fan whose sole interest is the TV in the RV

* Roger and Jessica: newlyweds who haven't consummated their vows yet, so watch out—they're a bit on edge

* Art and Gracie: friends of Millie and Lester's who double as canasta partners when life on the RV gets slow

* Renee Angelo: a former high school classmate of Mark and Claire's who supposedly is winning the RV for her grandma…or is it grandpa?

* Tawny: a makeup counter salesgirl who spends her days polishing her nails

* John Madison: a dad of two who wants the RV to go to Disneyland

* Aaron Jefferson: a doctor with a constantly beeping pager

* Milo Otis: a tired security guard

* Adele Williams: a teller at Lawford City Bank with a deadline

Chapter One

Claire Richards ran her hand along the sleek exterior, the smooth metal gliding beneath her palm. If only men were this well-equipped. And this useful.

Her fingers slipped down the glossy surface, up and over the body ridges. Perfect. Absolutely perfect. Now all she had to do was win the forty-five-foot-long beast. She'd worry about wrangling it down the highway later.

The shadow of the massive cream-and-burgundy Deluxe Motor Homes RV dwarfed Claire, even though she was five-foot-nine. The house on wheels had plenty of space for the bedroom, kitchen and living room, the sign advertised. Perfect, she repeated. A house and a getaway car all in one. She needed both—and the sooner the better. She'd made a promise and didn't have a lot of time left to keep it. Not nearly enough time.

But getting out of Mercy, Middle-of-Nowhere, Indiana, was about more than keeping a promise. No matter what, Claire was going to make the new start she needed. She'd given notice at the beauty shop, tucked most of her belongings into storage, and scraped up enough savings to fund her move. When Claire Richards leapt off a cliff, she did it without hesitation and without a safety net.

In the back of her mind, a tiny doubt whispered that changing her life was about more than physical distance. Claire quickly pushed the thought away.

The RV was her ticket to a new life in California and to the only family she had left. She gave the motor home a final pat, then crossed to the registration table.

"Is this where I sign up for a chance to win the RV?"

A cheerleader from Mercy High turned a clipboard toward Claire and handed her a pen. The girl had dark, bouncy hair and a thousand-watt smile that must have cost three dollars a watt at the orthodontist's. She wore a blue-and-white uniform and white sneakers. Change her hair to blond and she could have been Claire at that age.

"There's, like, a million people signed up and only, like, the first twenty get on." The girl gestured toward a board of rules. The number *20* shouted back at Claire, bold and big. "The contest starts Sunday. Try to be, like, early, and bring all your stuff." The cheerleader dipped her head and started filing her nails.

For a fleeting second, Claire felt like grabbing the girl's hand and telling her not to forgo a college education, not to put her faith in some silly boy who would end up working in the steel mill because his father worked there and jobs were inherited along with the family cowlick. She wanted to tell Go-Team-Go Gidget to get out of Mercy while she still had a chance. Or she'd find herself at twenty-eight, still single, stuck in this town and desperate enough to sign up for the September "Survive and Drive" contest at the mall.

Hoping for the opportunity to win back the freedom and hope she'd had in abundance at eighteen.

"Ma'am?"

That word jarred Claire back to reality. When had she gone from being a "miss" to a "ma'am"? Had there been some road sign she'd missed? *You are now entering middle age. It's all downhill from here.*

"Ma'am?" The girl said again. Her emery board stilled. "Did you, like, want to sign up?"

"Yes, yes." Claire scribbled her name on the sheet, then handed it to the girl. She circled the RV again, working on a strategy. There would be nearly two dozen people fighting for the vehicle. She'd better start humming the theme song to *Rocky*. She'd need to prepare for a long haul inside this house on wheels, competing with a bunch of strangers, or worse, people she actually knew.

"I wouldn't mind being stuck inside an RV with a beauty like you," said a deep voice Claire recognized.

Mark Dole, brother to Nate, Jack, Luke and Katie. A man Claire knew too well. The Doles had been neighbors of Claire's nearly all her life. Ever since they'd been kids, Mark and Claire had fought and played like brother and sister. One day, they'd be friends making sand castles and the next, they'd be slinging mud balls at one other. Two hot-tempered people who brought out the worst in each other.

Claire turned around. "Hi, Mark."

He had the same slightly wavy hair she remembered, dark brown with a hint of golden highlights, like some sun god. He was athletic, muscular but not bulky, and had been blessed with brilliant blue eyes that seemed to bore right through a girl. Mark Dole was the closest thing Mercy had to a Calvin Klein cover model. A man like him—gorgeous and full of pickup lines—should come with a warning label.

"Claire! I didn't know that was you. I thought—" She

saw him cut off the sentence before he said something stupid such as he'd mistaken her for someone he stood a chance with.

That would never happen. Once, Claire's best friend Jenny, who was dating Nate Dole, had·thought it would be fun to double with Claire and Mark. The results had been disastrous. The boy who'd dipped her ponytail in blue tempera paint in third grade hadn't become boyfriend material. They'd clashed on everything from the movie choice to the popcorn tub size. They'd ended up with their own buckets, sitting on the far flanks of Jenny and Nate.

"What are you doing here?" Claire asked.

"I'm signing up for the competition. I'm going to out-last all the other poor suckers and win this baby for my-self." He gave the hull a self-assured pat.

He was the epitome of all the men she'd vowed to avoid. Men full of sweet lines and sexy words, but lacking considerably in substance and permanence. Men who wouldn't just break her heart—they'd feed the pieces to a shredder.

One of Claire's close friends, Leanne Hartford, had learned that firsthand after dating Mark for two months, falling half in love with him, and then being unceremoniously dumped just before the senior prom. Claire had never forgotten—nor forgiven—Mark's insensitive end to the relationship.

Claire forced herself not to gag. "Poor suckers?"

"Well, the other people who signed up. There's probably only a few anyway."

"Try closer to, like, a million." She did her best to mimic the cheerleader. "Only the first twenty get on." She pointed out the sign.

He blinked. "That many?"

"A contest like this is a major deal in Mercy. Plus, it's

a chance at a free ride out of small-town life. You'd have to be nuts not to gamble on it." Claire had done more than take a chance, but she didn't tell Mark.

He considered that a moment, then looked at her. Those cobalt eyes had probably made a lot of women's hearts beat faster, but Claire was not impressed. Eyes were eyes, even if they were an almost electric color. "What about you?"

"My name's already on the list."

"Oh." He nodded, then flicked a thumb at the RV. "So, you think you can outlast *me?*"

"I know I can."

"Want to bet?"

"Sure. Twenty bucks says I win this thing."

"Sounds fair." He grinned. "I bet you're out of there on the first day."

She let out a chuff of disbelief. "You won't last the first night. Remember, you'll be sharing a bathroom *and* a mirror."

He clutched his heart. "Oooh, that's low. You wound me, Claire."

Despite everything, Claire laughed. If there was one talent Mark had always had, it was the ability to make her laugh. "Hey, if those arrows work, I have a million more, baby." She crossed her arms over her chest and shifted her weight into fighter stance. "I am going to outlast you, Mark Dole. And then I'm going to drive away from this town and leave you in my dust."

"I think you're the one who'll be choking on my exhaust." He raised an eyebrow and gave her a lopsided smile. "You don't know who you're messing with."

"Neither do you. Never underestimate the stubbornness of a woman." Especially a woman with virtually everything at stake. Claire spun on her heel and started to walk away.

"Claire! You've forgotten one thing," Mark called.

She stopped, pivoted back. "What?"

He pointed at her, then himself. "You. Me. Locked together in there." He gestured toward the RV and smirked. "It could get mighty hot."

"Yeah, I'm feeling lukewarm already."

He stepped closer. The woodsy scent of his cologne drifted between them. On any other man, it would have been sexy, tempting, but on Mark—

"We're not teenagers anymore, you know," he said, the deep timbre of his voice a reminder of how far along Mark was on the male development scale. "We're all grown up, with very grown-up desires. Knowing how stubborn both of us are, we could be in there for a *very* long time. Aren't you worried such tight quarters might, ah…tempt you?"

She fanned her face à la Scarlett O'Hara. "Why Mr. Dole, I do declare, you are the most seductive thing I've ever seen. How will I ever keep my head on straight?"

"Cute. Very cute." He stepped back. "We'll see who's the last one off the fun bus there."

"I already know that answer. Me." She took a step closer to him, pointing at his chest. "And remember, I don't play fair."

"Neither do I, Claire." His smile reached his eyes. If she'd been any other woman, it might have made her pulse skitter. "This is going to be fun."

From the smoldering look in his gaze, she knew he wasn't talking about the kind of fun they'd had playing Twister when they were seven. Something in Claire's gut coiled with heat.

Nothing a cold soda wouldn't fix, she told herself, and walked away. Well, maybe two cold sodas.

Earsplitting buzzing, screaming bleats. In his ear. Loud, annoying, *repetitive* sound. Mark slapped at the night-stand, searching blindly for the source of the god-awful noise. He bumped against hard plastic and smacked it un-til his fingers hit the snooze button.

He cracked open an eye and glanced at the red num-bers. Three in the morning. What insane person gets up that early?

He rolled back to the pillow and closed his eyes. When he did, the image of the RV flashed in his mind. He jerked upright. "I'm that insane person," he grumbled.

The Survive and Drive contest started today. Only the first twenty got on the RV. If he didn't haul his butt out of bed and get to the mall, he'd lose his shot.

He stumbled for the shower and didn't bother to wait for hot water. He stripped off his boxers, stepped inside the stall and let the needles of cold water sting him awake. Two minutes of sudsing and rinsing and he was done. He rushed through the rest of his morning routine, choosing the faster electric razor over the more-precise disposable blade, skipping aftershave.

In his childhood bedroom, Mark flicked on the over-head light and got dressed in jeans and a T-shirt. Pennants from Indianapolis Colts and Pacers games hung on his walls, souvenirs of trips to the stadium with his dad. A selection of sports trophies collected cobwebs on a shelf on one wall, golden images of boys at play with footballs, hockey sticks and baseballs. A five-year-old picture of his family—Jack, Mark, Luke, Nate, Katie and their par-ents—sat on top of his dresser. Mark's gaze swept over it all. He ignored one corner, though. On that wall hung a plaque etched with many words of praise for Mark Dole.

And not a single one of them was true.

He shoved enough clothes for a few days into a gym bag, tossed in some deodorant, shaving cream, a razor and his toothbrush. He added his laptop, a notebook and a few pencils, then zipped it shut, slipped into his sneakers without untying them, and headed over to Luke's room.

His twin brother's bedroom was in sharp contrast to his own. Luke, the more organized of the two, had already turned his space into one befitting a grown-up. The few pieces of furniture he'd moved with him from his California house seemed to bring all the remnants of what had once been a happy home into the small space. The hallway light cast a soft glow over the room, revealing a handmade quilt on the corner recliner and a series of photos on the rolltop desk Mary had given Luke on his last birthday. The photos were of happier times, before Death had made a special delivery to Luke's door.

A sharp pang grabbed at Mark's chest. He was twenty-nine. Too old to be playing the games of his youth. He'd outgrown the pennants, the cheers of the crowd, the adoring girls standing on the sidelines. When Mary'd died last year, Mark had seen and felt—in some special twin synergy—Luke's grief and had suddenly known he was missing something very special. Coming home two weeks ago and being welcomed into his parents' warm, bread-scented home told him just what that missing part was.

A home. Not an apartment empty of anything but the basic necessities of bachelorhood. Not a string of women, their names blurred into one—CherylJudyMelanie-Heather. For the first time in his life, Mark wanted a taste of what his brother had had. He was done with fast food. He wanted roast turkey with all the trimmings.

But having that meant settling down. Being responsible. Not letting Luke down and losing their business in one fell swoop. Mark wasn't even sure he had it in him to be the kind of guy who could be counted on for a paycheck every two weeks and a retirement account.

Either way, before he thought about himself, he needed to restore Luke's life to him—or at least the parts Mark was able to give back, which meant getting to the mall before nineteen other people did. He shook Luke awake.

"What? Go away. I'm asleep."

"I need you to drop me off, or pick up my car later. I'm not leaving it in the mall lot. It could be there for days."

Luke let out a string of expletives that said he'd forgotten his promise to drive. "It's a *Nova,* Mark. Nobody's going to steal a damned beater box from the seventies."

"Hey, my car's a classic."

Luke rolled over and covered his head with the blankets. "Maybe it will be when disco comes back, but right now, it's just an old car." Luke let out a sigh. "I'll pick it up later."

"Thanks."

Luke peeled back the blankets from his face and blinked several times. "You really going to try to win that thing?"

"Yep."

"What the heck for?"

"I want to—" he stopped himself. "I want a portable house." Not a very good lie, as lies went, but he couldn't tell Luke the truth. Luke had been through enough this past year, more than anyone should have to endure. With any luck, Mark could fix some of that by being the last man standing in the RV.

And then, maybe he could embark on fixing his own

life. First, he'd have to figure out where to start on himself, though.

Luke shrugged, pulled up the blankets again. "Wake me when it's over."

Mark dashed out the door, hopped into his Nova and headed across town. Mercy had been growing over the last year as people in Lawford opted to leave the city for land and quiet. The population had stretched by a couple thousand, prompting the opening of a mall, even though it only encompassed twelve stores. Still, it seemed to stay busy, especially with the summer tourists and antiquers.

When Mark arrived, he counted eighteen cars in the main parking lot, a couple in the mall employee area. Damn. How early did these people get up? Once inside, he saw a virtual campground had been set up on the cold white tile of the courtyard. Lounge chairs, beach towels, blankets, pillows. And people—nineteen of them. With the motor home beside them, the whole pristine, antiseptic scene looked like Walt Disney's version of a campsite.

Mark settled onto the floor at the end of the line and rested his arms across his knees. On his left an elderly woman sat in one of those three-dollar folding lawn chairs. Beside her slept a nearly bald, wrinkled man. They both wore beret-style hats topped with a fat yarn pom-pom. The old woman was knitting, her needles clacking away in the quiet. Her husband had his head back, mouth open, loud, hock-hock-hock snores coming from his mouth.

"Why hello, sonny. I'm Millie Parsons. Are you here to win the motor home?" she asked, without missing a stitch.

"Yes, I am."

She reached out a gnarled hand and patted his. "Good luck, dear." She smiled nicely, then added, "but Lester and I are planning on winning it. We want to go to Florida, don't you know.'' She grinned until all her dentures showed. ''And we don't plan on losing.''

Mark smiled right back at her. ''Neither do I.''

Her smile dropped away, she yanked her hand away and went back to her knitting. Click, clack, click, clack. Row after row of pink stitches. Probably making a noose for anyone who tried to outlast her and Lester.

A very unladylike curse sounded from behind him. Mark turned and saw Claire. ''I'm twenty-one,'' she said.

''Honey, you couldn't pass for it,'' Mark quipped. But in reality, she could. Her straight blond hair was up in a ponytail, a youthful style fitting her smooth, unlined skin. She had bright, almost emerald eyes, and a generous mouth he'd never seen without red lipstick. From ten feet away, it screamed ''Kiss Me.'' That is, it did to every man but Mark, who had never been her favorite male Homo sapiens.

She was one of the tallest women he knew, lean and athletic, and given to tight, bright-pink jeans and iridescent tanks that never seemed to extend past her belly button. God bless clothing designers who didn't account for long torsos. Catching a glimpse of the creamy skin above her waistband could become his favorite pastime. She'd finished off the outfit with boots sporting three-inch heels. There was a name for shoes like that, but he wasn't going to say it in public.

Claire didn't seem to appreciate his lusty appraisal. In fact, she gave him a most irritated look. ''I'm not talking about my age. I meant my place in line. I'll never get on there now.''

He blew on his finger like a gunfighter who'd knocked out the competition. ''Gee, that was an easy bet to win.''

Mark had always wondered what a glower looked like. He knew now—and it wasn't pretty.

"It's not over yet," she said. "Some of these people might be here to keep the others company." She dropped her large suitcase to the floor and plopped down beside it.

"Who are you? Ginger? Taking along a year's worth of clothes for a three-hour tour?"

"I'd rather come over-prepared than find out two days into this that I don't have any deodorant. I might be here for days."

Mark leaned over and whispered in her ear. "If you want to outlast Lester and his girl here, it might be *weeks*. She's got a lot of knitting to do."

A faint smile appeared on Claire's face. "I'm prepared." She arched an eyebrow at his small gym bag. "Are you?"

"I travel light."

"Then travel out of here and give me your place in line."

"Claire, darling, you almost sound desperate."

A flicker of something—fear, worry—flashed in her eyes, but in an instant, she was all Claire again. "No, just determined." She fidgeted for a few seconds. Then she dug in her handbag and pulled out a bag of Hershey Kisses. She unwrapped two and popped one in her mouth. She offered the bag to him.

He shook his head. "A little early in the morning for a sugar high."

"It's never too early, or too late, for chocolate." She popped in the second, chewed, swallowed. "Give me your place in line. I *need* that RV."

"So do I," Mark said. "Now, move over, twenty-one, and give the big boys some room."

She crossed her arms over her knees. "I don't think so."

He crossed his over his chest. "I figured as much."

They sat there like two store mannequins for the better part of an hour. A few other people hiked into the mall, suitcases and duffel bags in hand. All but two young boys turned away once they ran a count on those ahead of them. The boys settled down beside Claire and got into a mock sparring match.

At 5:00 a.m., a thin, wiry woman who looked like a steel rail came out from the mall offices, stood before the group and clapped her hands. "Okay, group, let's begin!" She had a long, pinched face and black hair cut short enough for Mark to see her ears. He could imagine her as a gym teacher somewhere, shouting tortuous instructions with exuberance.

Lester continued hock-hocking away. His wife gave him a jab in the side. He jerked awake, blinking and looking around as though he had no idea where he was or why his wife had done that. "Is it time, Millie?"

"Shush." Millie tucked her knitting needles into an I Love Bingo canvas bag. "Pay attention to the lady, Lester."

Millie probably cut Lester's meat into little pieces before dinner. She seemed the type.

"I'm Nancy Lewis, the community development coordinator for the Mercy Mall. We may be small, but we're growing," she said cheerily, using the trademark sign-off for the mall. Nancy smiled perkily and paced along the line. "I'd like to welcome you to the Survive and Drive contest! Only twenty of you will get the chance to win this fantastic motor home." She ran her hand along the hull with the reverence of one of Bob Barker's girls. "It's a very expensive vehicle—an eighty-five-thousand-dollar value. It has a fully-equipped kitchen with gorgeous wood cabinets, a lounge chair, sofa, queen bed and dinette. We've added a couple of fold-up stools to provide additional seating. There are three televisions, one up front, one in the living area, and one in the bedroom. The shower comes with a power massage head and a skylight. Power windows, power locks and deluxe stereo system.'' She slipped her hand along the side in a swoosh finale. ''Anyone would be thrilled to take this motoring up to the Catskills or down the coast of Florida.''

Millie gave Lester another jab; he'd started to doze again. Claire, however, was paying close attention. Her gaze flicked between the RV and the woman, her muscles tensed, ready to spring should the number of contestants get stretched to twenty-one.

''I'd like to thank Deluxe Motor Homes for donating this magnificent RV. They're celebrating their fiftieth anniversary in business here in Mercy by giving away one of their newest models. Let's give a big thanks to Don Nash, the CEO of Deluxe.''

From the front of the vehicle came Don himself, a slight man in a tailored suit. Deluxe Motor Homes was one of the biggest employers in town and did a brisk business creating custom RVs for country singers and retirees. Mark supposed this contest promotion was a drop in their marketing budget bucket.

Led by Nancy's wild bring-back-Tinkerbell-from-the-dead claps, the crowd applauded Don's generous donation.

''Now.'' Nancy clapped her hands together again. Mark wondered if her palms were starting to smart. ''Let's play who's who among the competition before we board.'' She pointed to the first person in line. ''Why don't you start?''

Mark craned his neck around Millie and Lester's lawn

chairs. A thin African-American woman wearing business clothes sat primly on one of the mall benches someone had dragged over by the RV. "I'm Adele Williams."

"And…" Nancy prompted, waving her hand in a circular motion. "What do you do?"

"I'm a loan officer for Lawford First National."

"Probably could have bought her own RV," muttered Millie. She pulled out her knitting again. It seemed to be the thing she did when she was frustrated. Click, clack, click, clack.

Nancy went down the line and unearthed a few people Mark knew, a few he didn't. There was John Madison, a guy he'd played football with. John was married and had two kids, a fact he gleefully shared, complete with photos. "They want to go to Disney World," he said. "Two little kids, dreaming of Mickey." He glanced around but no one expressed an iota of empathy.

There was Renee Angelo, a girl who'd been a class behind Mark. She told Nancy she wanted the RV so her grandmother could "retire in style." Again, not an ounce of pathos from the group.

Then two makeup counter salesgirls, a security guard who looked about a hundred years old, three women who were stay-at-home moms and one guy who didn't seem to have a job and couldn't come up with a good reason for wanting the RV. "This girl asked me if I wanted to sign up," he said with a shrug. "So I did."

Then there was the bingo bunch, two couples about Millie and Lester's age, who all talked of moving to Florida for the winter months. Millie apparently knew these folks and muttered about them under her breath as she click-clacked away. Number fifteen was a doctor. He checked his beeper twice while telling Nancy about his practice. Mark didn't think he'd last long.

Claire was mute. She watched Nancy make her way down the line, eyeing them all like the second-ranked runner warily watching the first-ranked before the race's start.

Sixteen and seventeen were a married couple on their honeymoon. They must be insane to want to spend their honeymoon in an RV with a bunch of strangers. They looked young and gullible, still at the age where they thought the world was going to hand them good things on a platter. A few short months ago, Mark had felt the same way. Funny how fast things could change.

Eighteen and nineteen were Millie and Lester. Twenty was Mark. When Nancy asked him what he did for work, he hesitated. "I'm…I was a salesman for a software development company but now I write training manuals."

"How cool! Like for Microsoft?"

He snorted. "Not exactly."

"And why do you want to win the RV, Mark?" Nancy flashed him a smile.

"I, ah…" What could he say? He was dead broke, he'd screwed up royally and he needed the RV to provide himself with both a reliable ride to California and a means to right the mistakes he'd made? Instead, he said the first thing that came to mind. "I want to go to Disneyland."

"How sweet," Nancy stepped over by Claire, then counted with her pointer finger. "I'm sorry, you're twenty-one."

"But I couldn't pass for it," Claire joked, using Mark's one-liner as if trying to charm Nancy into letting her stay. "I'm Claire—"

"You're *twenty-one*," Nancy interrupted. "The rules say only twenty get on. Sorry." She pointed to the board of rules. Then she walked back to the head of the line. "Okay, people." She clapped twice. "Bags up! Let's get aboard!"

Millie jabbed Lester again and stood while he folded their chairs and hoisted their bags. The others who'd missed being part of the lucky twenty wandered away.

Mark turned back to Claire. He'd never seen such a forlorn look in a woman's eyes before. "I'm sorry, Claire."

"Give me your place." She gripped his arm. "Please, Mark. I've never asked a favor of you before, just give me this one thing and I'll…" he saw her reach for the words, knowing from past history Claire wasn't the type to ask anyone for anything, "owe you for the rest of my life."

He hesitated. Any other day, if a pretty woman asked a favor of him, he'd oblige, charmingly offering a date in trade. They'd wine, dine, flirt, and before the end of the night, she'd be in his bed and he'd figure he'd been the winner.

But this wasn't any other day. And these weren't ordinary circumstances. For the first time in his life, Mark Dole was desperate. Desperate enough to ignore a beautiful woman's smile and deny her the one thing she wanted. "I can't, Claire. Sorry."

Disbelief washed over her features. "You can't tell me your trip to *Disneyland* is more important than my reasons."

"And just why do you want to win that thing? It's a bit big for your driveway, don't you think?"

"I need to get to California." She said it with such determination that he doubted she was lying.

"Buy a plane ticket."

"A plane ticket doesn't solve my problems. Besides, up until yesterday, I was a hairdresser at Flo's Cut and Go. I'm rolling in blue hair dye and quarter tips, not dough.'' Her gaze filled with entreaty again. ''Please, Mark. I know you haven't always liked me, but—''

''Who says I don't like you?''

''All aboard!'' Nancy cried. ''Last call for the RV Train, bound for Florida or maybe Disneyland.''

Mark ignored the drill instructor. ''Who says I don't like you?'' he repeated.

''Come on, Mark. We had the date from hell with Jenny and Nate. Don't you remember? We fought over everything.''

He smiled. His memories included a spirited fight, yes, but also a spirited attraction. Why they'd never pursued that, he couldn't recall. ''I remember you were pretty warm that night.''

She let out a sigh. ''That wasn't me. It was the butter at the bottom of your popcorn bucket.'' She shook her head. ''That's not the point. I need to get on that RV and win it.''

Mark raised his hands in a gesture of futility. ''Sorry, Claire. I wish I could help you.'' He picked up his bag, and crossed to the motor home. Behind him, he could almost hear the sound of Claire's disappointment.

He'd arrived before her. He was number twenty. He'd earned his place on the motor home. But as he walked toward the prize he intended to win, he couldn't have felt like a bigger heel if he'd been on the bottom of a pair of loafers.

Chapter Two

Claire clutched her suitcase and watched Mark climb the first step of the RV. She hated him and envied him and wanted to throw things at him, but truth was, she had arrived here one person too late. She'd blown her chance because she'd stayed on the phone too long. A few too many minutes of conversation with the nurse. And now she was left holding a suitcase, with no way to get to the coast. To her new life. To the first person she could call family in a long time.

Buy a plane ticket, Mark had said. If only it were that simple. She'd made a promise, and now, damn it all and damn it again, she was going to have to break it. And even worse, do so over the phone, with one end of the connection on a cell phone in Mercy and the other end in a room in California smelling of antiseptic.

Despair settled over her, heavy and thick. She'd come so far, risked so much, and now she was going to lose it all. Had she really thought she could pull this off? Change her life with a risky move like this?

She dropped the suitcase to the floor, sat down on top and buried her face in her hands. She would not cry. She would not—

"I can't do it! It's so small! I can't—" One of the makeup-counter salesgirls came barreling off the RV, nearly knocking Mark over in her rush to flee. "It's like a coffin in there!" She stopped in the courtyard, took in several deep gulps of air, then ran out of the mall.

"One down," Nancy said. "Eighteen to go and we'll have a winner."

"No, wait!" Claire scrambled to her feet, grabbed her suitcase, and ran over to Nancy. "The last person hasn't gotten on yet. Technically, the competition hasn't started. And now, you only have nineteen. The rules said twenty."

Nancy's mouth turned in and she narrowed her gaze. "I can count. We had twenty, now we have nineteen."

"The rules said—"

"The lady's right." Mark interrupted, still standing on the step. He flashed Nancy a winning smile. "I can see you're a nice person, someone…understanding. She just wants a chance." He indicated Claire. "You seem the kind who would give her one." He leaned closer to Nancy. "Between you and me, I don't think she'll last more than a few hours anyway. Then you'll be back to nineteen again, all before the mall opens. Besides," he added on a whisper, "she might sue. It's a sticky situation, considering I haven't gotten on yet."

Why would Mark help her? Especially after he'd turned her down earlier? Claire didn't bother to try to understand his motives, not when her chance at boarding the RV was at stake.

The lawsuit implication seemed to sway Nancy. "Okay, get on. But remember," she cautioned before

Claire took a step, "I'm being very nice in giving you this chance."

"Nancy, you're all heart." Mark flashed his best smile. It worked its usual magic, a trick Claire had seen a thousand times in the years she'd known Mark. He smiled and grown women swooned. Even hard-nosed Nancy melted—she returned his smile with a little giggle.

"Thank you." Claire shook Nancy's hand but the other woman barely noticed. Her gaze was entirely on Mark, until she was interrupted by a question from Don Nash and turned away with clear reluctance. "Let's get in there, Mark."

"Ladies first," he said, gesturing before him.

Claire shook her head. "I know how you are. You just want to watch my butt. Get in there and I'll watch yours instead."

He arched an eyebrow. "I didn't know you liked me. Or my rear, Claire." Mark wasted a smile on her. Claire felt a flutter in her stomach that surely had to come from the three donuts she'd gobbled on her way out the door. He reached into his pocket and withdrew a pencil. "Here." He handed it to her.

"What's this for?"

"In case you want to capture the view." Then he climbed the steps and entered the RV. Claire sighted her target and launched. Perfect aim. The pencil beaned his left temple.

"Hey!" Mark said.

Claire grinned. "I told you I don't play fair."

He leaned toward her. "Makes it all that much more interesting, doesn't it?" There were a hundred other implications in his voice. She chose to ignore them all.

Once inside, Claire understood why the claustrophobic girl had run screaming from the motor home. Twenty people, with luggage, did not fit easily in a forty-five-foot trailer, no matter how nicely decorated the interior. Already, the air was stifling, filled with the odor of humans and the sickly-sweet stench of perfume. If Claire hadn't had so much at stake herself, she would have left, too. The crowd was overwhelming.

Nancy entered the RV and grimaced. "Now that we're all here, let's start the competition." She flicked a switch at the front of the vehicle and blessed cool air began to pump through the vents. "First, a few rules. The newspaper will be delivered daily and you can get local channels on the TVs, so you'll stay current. There's a full kitchen, with a stocked refrigerator and food cabinet. I'll be bringing by fresh groceries, as often as they're needed with a crowd this big. Just give me a list and I'll do my best. A couple of area restaurants have graciously agreed to donate dinners for the next few nights. In exchange for a mention in the media coverage, of course."

"Media coverage?" someone asked from the back.

"Oh yeah, didn't I tell you? A crew from Ten-Spot News in Lawford will be out later today to film you. Sort of "The Real World/Survivor" in an RV. It was part of what convinced Deluxe to donate the RV. Anyway, Ten-Spot will be poking their heads in here from time to time. They're on their way over right now. There was an accident on the interstate and they got delayed. So they missed the big boarding." Nancy tapped a finger against her lips. "Maybe we could re-stage that, for the cameras." She shook her head. "Anyway, back to the rules. You'll all be in here with each other for a while, so be nice. No profanity, no lewd gestures," she shot a glance at Mark that seemed to say she wouldn't mind a lewd gesture from him later, "and no fighting. Sleeping will be a first-come, first-served kind of thing. There's a queen bed in back, a double in the fold-out couch, another double on top of the cab and a recliner. The captain's chairs up front are pretty comfortable, too. And then there's the floor.'' She tapped her foot against it. ''Carpeted at least.''

Nancy went on to say that if they left the RV, they'd be disqualified. Stepping outside the vehicle for any reason was considered quitting. The competition would go on as long as there was more than one person inside. ''Last to go takes the RV home,'' she said, sweeping her hand around the room like Vanna White. ''That's it. Any questions?''

''How many hours do you think this will take?'' Adele asked.

Nancy shrugged. ''I don't know. In the contest at Mall of America, there were two guys who lasted three months.''

A gasp went up from the crowd. Adele glanced at her watch. ''I have to be at work by noon or use up a vacation day.''

Nancy gave her an indulgent smile, as if Adele were slow-witted. ''I think you'll be here past noon.''

Adele glanced around the crowded room, then sat on one of the kitchenette chairs. ''I'll have to call my boss.''

''There's no phone in the RV. If you have a cell phone, you can use that. Otherwise, the only contact with the outside world will be through me.'' She smiled graciously at them all. ''I'd be glad to let your family know how you're doing, or they could come by and visit while they shop, and talk to you through the window. Be sure to tell them that Joe's Camping Store is having a big sale this week on camping gear, to go along with our promotion.'' When no one else asked a question, Nancy gave them a little wave, wished them luck and got off the RV.

Claire saw clear relief in Nancy's face when she took

in a deep breath of canned mall air. When the door shut, Claire felt a twinge of panic. Nineteen other people. One RV. For days on end. What had she just gotten herself into? And what if it didn't work out?

Mark's gaze caught hers. "You okay?"

She drew herself up and took a breath. "Of course."

"Of course," he repeated with a smile that said he knew she was lying.

"I think everyone should stow their luggage in the bedroom," Millie, the knitting grandma, said. "Lester, take our things back there."

"Who made you boss?" said Roger, who'd just gotten married on Friday. He was only twenty-one, too young to be married, Claire thought. She'd cut his hair last week. Flat top, shaved sides, à la the marines. She couldn't believe he'd talked his new wife, Jessica, into spending their honeymoon on the RV. She supposed it was better than spending the weekend at Jessica's mom's house, probably the only other option they could afford. Not exactly an auspicious beginning for married life, but Claire understood being blind to everything but love. Blind to a lack of money, blind to a lack of a job. Blind as a stupid bat, flying face-first into a wall of denial.

Millie pursed her lips. "Do you have a better idea, son?"

"Well, no." Roger looked flustered by her challenge. "I think we should decide things by committee, though."

Millie let out a sigh. "There is very little room in here, in case you didn't notice. If we stow our bags in the bedroom, we have a private place to change our clothes."

"Okay," Roger said. For the next few minutes, there was nothing but the sounds of grunts and "excuse me's" as each of them made their way to the bedroom and deposited their luggage.

"Well," Millie said when they were done. "Anyone up for a game of canasta?"

The silence that greeted her made it clear how the crowd felt about card games. Somebody started a pot of coffee in the tiny kitchen. One of the men—Danny, the one who didn't seem to have a job, Claire remembered— flopped into the driver's seat, grabbed the satellite remote and turned on the TV. Typical.

"Awesome! I can watch every game in the country." Danny immediately put the remote to use. A half second on each station until he knew exactly where ESPN and Fox Sports were located. Then he settled back in the chair and propped his feet on the dash to watch football.

"Glad you got on the bus to nowhere now?" Mark asked, coming up beside her in the corner she'd ducked into to stay out of the crush of people.

Lord, he was awfully close. Claire stiffened, trying to take up less space. "Of course."

"Seems like it will be close quarters for a while. Think you can stand that?"

"Can you?"

"Oh yeah." He leaned toward her. She could feel his breath tickling along her collarbone. "I like being close."

She pulled herself away, as far as she could, which was about three inches. It was nowhere near enough distance. "Seems you're not the only one." She gestured toward Roger and Jessica.

The newlyweds had commandeered the sofa and stretched out along the length of it. They were half entwined with each other and had already started on the honeymoon. Loud, sloppy sounds of kissing came from their corner.

"That's not making love," Mark said with disdain. "That's wrestling."

Laughter burst from Claire. The moment of détente felt good, the laughter a much-needed break in the tension she'd been feeling ever since she threw out her old life, sure the new one was just a matter of waiting out the rest of the competitors. But now she didn't feel so confident about her decision.

Millie hurried over to the couch and rapped the surface with her knitting needle. Roger and Jessica broke apart and sat up. "There'll be none of that," Millie said, wagging her finger at them. "It's disgusting."

"Come on, grandma. We just got married yesterday." Roger held up Jessica's left hand as proof.

"Then get a room at the Motel 6. This is not the place for...for *that*."

"We're taking this RV on our honeymoon," Roger said.

"*When* you win it, that's when your honeymoon begins. Until then, I think you should sleep up front and your girl should sleep in the back, on the floor. Lester and I will have the bed and we can keep an eye on her."

"Hey," piped up Danny. "Who says you get the big bed?"

"Lester and I are the oldest," she said, as if that settled it.

"No you aren't, Millie," called one of the other elderly people. "My Gracie here has six months on you." That started another spirited disagreement about birth dates, which led into a game of one-upmanship about whose hip was worse and who deserved the bed more, based on their medical files.

Mark squeezed into the center of the room. "I have a fair way of deciding who gets the beds," he shouted over the din.

Claire glanced up in surprise. Since when did Mark get

involved in anything besides his own life? He'd never been the kind of guy to step into the middle of a mess. In high school, he'd always been content to ride the popularity wave. Now he was helping her, negotiating a sleeping peace treaty and generally acting like a nice guy—not like the Mark she remembered. Since he'd returned from California, something had changed. For good? Claire doubted it. Men like Mark didn't make permanent personality changes.

Everyone quieted down and looked at Mark. He grabbed the deck of cards on the kitchen table. Millie opened her mouth to protest. "I only need them for a minute," Mark said. He shuffled the deck and then held it aloft. "There's sleeping for six in the beds, then two captain's chairs and the recliner here in the living room. That makes nine comfortable places to sleep. Everyone takes a card. Highest cards get first pick. Tomorrow night, we deal again, so you always have a shot at a bed."

There were a few grumbles, but no one disagreed. Mark circled the RV, letting each person take a card. He smiled when he got to Claire. "Maybe you'll get a joker."

"Already had one of those, thank you." She took the first card from the deck. A jack of clubs. She stood a good chance at a comfortable place to sleep. After the sleepless night she'd had, it was a welcome thought.

"I got an ace," Millie crowed when Mark got to her. "Lester, what'd you get?"

He flashed a two of diamonds. Millie's face fell. "I can't sleep with another man. It would be—"

"There's always the chairs," Mark said as he took his own card from the deck. He looked at it, put it in his back pocket, then laid the rest of the deck back on the table. "Now, let's divvy up the beds."

Millie immediately claimed a captain's chair, bemoaning that she would have to sleep without Lester. Adele Williams had a king of hearts, but gave it back. "It's after eleven. I can't lose my job over this thing, not if I don't know for sure I'll win. I better get to work." She grabbed her bag and headed out the door.

Eighteen people left for Claire to beat now. The loss of one person did nothing to open up space and air in the RV, but it was a beginning. Maybe after a night of sleeping on the floor, others would leave, too. The doctor had already been paged twice and looked anxious. He'd clearly thought the competition would be easy and quick. The three stay-at-home moms had shared a cell phone to call home and check on their kids. One looked ready to leave. Her little Jimmy had fallen off the swing set and scraped his knee. Claire could hear her debating whether to stay.

"Claire, what have you got?" Mark's voice drew her back to the card.

"A jack."

"You get next pick. There's space with Milo, the security guard, on the queen bed in back. Or a space beside Tawny, the other makeup girl, on the sofa bed. Or…" he reached into his back pocket and withdrew a queen. "Or a space beside me in the double bed over the cab."

She wondered if Mark had cheated, purposely taking a higher card than her own so he could end up in bed with her. Nah. That was a crazy thought. She and Mark barely tolerated each other. They only bordered on being friends because they'd grown up together, which meant they had skinned knees and mud pies in common, not desire. They might joke about an attraction, but there was nothing between them to worry about.

Still, she wasn't going to tinker with that by sharing a bed with him. She was through making stupid mistakes because a sexy smile overrode her better sense. Claire crossed the room and handed her jack to Lester.

"Thank you, missy." He clutched the card in his gnarled, wrinkled hand. "That's very kind of you."

"Lester, choose the chair beside me," Millie cried.

He ignored his wife. "I think I'll take some space in that bed right there." Lester pointed to the sofa bed.

"I am not sleeping with an old man!" Tawny got to her feet.

Millie bustled over and switched her card with the girl's, before she could protest. "Then you sleep up front, dear, in the chair, and I'll keep my Lester company."

Lester let out a heavy sigh.

By the time the rest of the beds had been accounted for, Claire realized Mark hadn't used his queen after all. He'd just tucked it back into the deck and moved on to the next person. She didn't ponder his reasoning. Better to leave it alone.

After lunch, Claire settled into the recliner, cracked open her journal and began to write.

Only fifteen people left. The doctor's gone, and so is one of the elderly couples, who opted to drive to Florida. The third mom left, to give little Jimmy a dose of TLC. If this keeps up, I'll win in no time. Danny, though, is glued to the chair and the TV. Millie, Lester, Art and Gracie are playing the world's longest card game. Tawny started a miniriot when she polished her nails and the fumes became toxic. The security guard, Milo, is snoring on the couch. Renee and John are reading, the others are talking quietly. Roger and Jessica are on the other end of the couch, looking quite unhappy for newlyweds. And Mark…

Claire stopped writing and closed the book. Mark...Well, he wasn't acting like the Mark she knew. He'd been a peacemaker, stepping in when tempers started to flare, proposing ideas to settle everything from bathroom time to washing dishes. He was diplomatic and charming enough that everyone listened. If she hadn't known him and his reputation for breaking hearts already, Claire would have probably found that...attractive. Either way, a relationship didn't figure into her future, so she dropped the thought of Mark like a hot coal.

It was after ten now in California. Claire dug her cell phone out of her suitcase and headed into the only private place within the RV—the bathroom. The reception was terrible, even with her antenna up, so she climbed inside the corner shower and stretched it toward the skylight. Marginally better.

The call took several seconds to connect. Finally, a ring. Then another. By the fourth ring, Claire was worried. Finally, on the fifth, a gravelly voice picked up. "Hello?"

"Dad? You okay?"

"Yeah, I was just wrestling with the nurse."

Claire laughed. "Who won?"

"I think I did, but she's already challenged me to a rematch." He paused to cough. The racking sounds were surely painful for him, but they also stabbed at Claire's chest, too. She wished to God she had a better plan. "Sorry, honey."

"You taking care of yourself?"

"As best I can." Another series of coughs hit him, this one blessedly shorter. "I wish I could see you."

Claire leaned her head against the cool tile wall of the shower. "Me, too, Dad."

David Sawyer was still just a voice to her. She had yet to hug her father, see how tall he was compared to her, see if his pinky finger had that same odd crook hers did. She'd only found her father four months ago, and already the demon called cancer was stealing him away.

He started coughing again and one of his visiting nurses, Jeannie, took the phone. "Hi, Claire." Over the last few weeks, these women, who maintained the physical link Claire didn't have, had become close friends, a tangible rope between herself and the father she was still getting to know.

"How is he?"

She heard Jeannie cup her hand over the phone. "As well as can be expected. The doctor said…" she hesitated, clearly wishing she could deliver this news in person, in one of those quiet rooms where relatives could grieve in privacy. "The surgery didn't quite get it all. He'll be starting chemotherapy in two weeks, as soon as he's recovered from the surgery. He can't go anywhere until it's done, but he should be feeling better soon."

The chemo, Claire knew, was no guarantee of anything. From the way her father sounded, it might not be the final cure he needed. "I'll be there soon."

If she didn't have possession of the RV by the time her father started chemo, she'd just grab a plane and figure out the rest of her life later. Her move, her new start—all of it would have to wait.

"They got most of it with the surgery and radiation, you know. It's still at stage two. With chemo—"

Claire's sigh finished the sentence. "I know."

"We're taking good care of him," Jeannie said. "He's not in a hospital, he's home. There's a lot of good news."

"I know. I appreciate all you're doing." In the background, Claire heard her father's coughs abate.

Weaker now, he came back on the phone. "Guess that's my cue to hang up. Talking wears me out."

Claire's hand gripped the phone tighter, as if she could hold him through the wireless connection. God, how she wanted to be there, to help him through this. "I know, Dad. Just take care of yourself. I'll be there soon."

"Are we..." he paused between words, searching for breath, "still going to...take that...vacation?"

Claire bit her lip. "Absolutely, Dad." She closed her eyes and hung on to the phone long after they'd said goodbye. A tear slipped down her face. Then another, until the stress and worry released itself in a sob. She who never cried, who could wither a cocky man with a glance, who had been the last to leave the beauty shop when the tornado five years ago came roaring through—she who had never cried as much in her life as she had in the last four months.

"Claire? You okay?" Mark had come into the bathroom and she hadn't even noticed. She must have forgotten to lock the door. "I knocked, but you didn't answer, and I heard you—"

She swiped away her tears and turned to face him, all Claire again. Well, herself taken down a notch. No matter how hard she tried lately, the spirited person she normally was had taken a back seat to someone a little more subdued, worried and unsure of her decisions.

"I'm fine. Just checking out the view from the skylight." She glanced up and saw plain, white mall ceiling. Twin recessed lights glared back at her. "Yep. It's a great view."

"You look upset. Is something wrong?"

"Nope. Not a thing." She tucked her phone into the back pocket of her jeans and stepped out of the shower.

He stopped her before she passed him. A zing of heat

went up her arm when he touched her. Must be her frazzled nerves. "Wait, don't go out there yet."

"Why not?"

"The TV crew is here. As soon as they showed up, three other people quit. Those two other moms took off—good thing, too, because their cell phone has been ringing nonstop with babysitters and husbands at work calling—then Milo left, saying he couldn't get a decent nap with all the commotion. So now we're down to twelve."

Eleven people to go before she had the RV. Some of them, like Millie, looked like they had every intention of spending weeks here. Claire Richards did not have weeks. She needed to win and get on the road to California, before she chickened out and ended up stuck at Flo's for the rest of her life. She needed this change, needed to embark on her *own* life, not the one she'd been suckered into by a guy who talked a good game.

And she needed to see her father, to spend time with him one-on-one and begin to recapture the years they'd lost. The doubts returned again to plague her mind. Could she make a new start? Did she really have it in her to chuck it all for something essentially unknown?

Either way, without the RV, making all of that happen would be near impossible. There weren't many options.

"You might want to put on your game face before you go out there," Mark was saying. "The reporter wants to interview everyone, find out why they're here, what their strategy is."

For the briefest second, she was tempted to lean against Mark, pour her troubles into his hands. To rely on someone else for once. Claire had been on her own for so long. The burden of being strong was suddenly too heavy.

He was so close. Inches from her.

Granted, it wasn't his fault. This wasn't exactly the

bathroom at the Taj Mahal. It was only slightly bigger than the bathroom in the two-bedroom ranch where she'd grown up. But never in that bathroom, or in any other, had she been more aware of the rise and fall of a man's chest. She shook herself back to reality. This was *Mark*.

"...and I'll warn you, they're looking for dirt," he said. "Ups the ratings, you know."

Claire gestured toward the shower. "I just came from there. No dirt on me." She tried to work up a laugh, but it fell flat.

Something dark and fierce simmered in his gaze, but his voice was all light and teasing, the same Mark she'd known all her life. "Doesn't look like you got all the important parts," he said. He ran a finger over the curve of her shoulder and she felt the heat ratchet up ten degrees. She'd never reacted like that to Mark before. Then again, the last time they'd "played" together, they'd both been nine. "You really should get naked to take a shower properly, you know."

"So I've heard." She needed some air. It wasn't his finger teasing along the edge of her tank that had her forgetting her name and where she was and what day it was. "Well, I better get back out there." But she didn't move.

Mark's face, so familiar, yet so different now that he had the angular lines and dusting of stubble of a grown man, was a breath away. "Any time you need someone to scrub your back or want to scrub mine," he smiled and some of the heat left his gaze as he kidded with her, "I have this spot right here..." he pointed to a place on his back, "that I can't reach by myself. If you'd care to help, the shower looks big enough for two."

Whoa. This was going into territory where Claire refused to journey. This was *Mark,* she reminded herself again. She knew, from all the years she'd lived around the corner from him, that he had as much interest in monogamy as a goldfish. She was twenty-eight and no longer interested in serial dating. Besides, she wasn't Mark's type—she wasn't young or buxom.

If he was making a pass at her, he had one of only two reasons in mind. He was hard up, or he was using this as some kind of strategy to win the RV. He'd weave his spell and convince her to get off. She wasn't giving up her dream to some guy with a soft touch and a good smile. She'd done that once before, for Travis. And had ended up stuck with a lease and a pile of bills while he pursued his dreams. Never again. "Thanks, but no thanks."

She started to brush past him. "Claire—"

Claire wheeled around. "I know you, Mark. I know your pattern. A night in your bed, maybe three. The sex would be oh-so-good." She ran a finger up his chest, her mouth exaggerating the *O*'s in her words. "We'd be peeling ourselves off the ceiling after we were done. And then, when you realized I actually had a *brain* above my breasts, you'd walk away. No," she put a finger to her chin. "You'd *run*. And I'd have wasted a few days of my life with a guy who can't see past my lingerie. I've been there, done that and have no intentions of being that stupid again, with you or any other man. So let me put you out of your misery and save us all grief down the road." She pulled the tank to the right, exposing the thin strap of her bra. "This set's blue, fringed with lace. The one I'll wear tomorrow is black. Then maybe I'll wear the red, or the indigo. Happy?" She slipped the shirt back. "Now, let's get back to the competition."

She stalked out of the bathroom, leaving Mark Dole with his jaw on the floor.

Chapter Three

Mark gave Claire two minutes, then he emerged from the bathroom and ducked into the bedroom, grabbing his laptop. If anyone had noticed they'd been in there at the same time, they didn't say a word. They were too immersed in their chance at fifteen minutes of fame. Or in the case of Ten-Spot News, more like fifteen seconds.

It was like a scene out of some cheap detective story. The bright light, the nosy journalist, the mike in someone's face. And the crowd in the motor home was eating it up. Mark had had his moment years ago and hated every second of it. The last thing he wanted was a repeat. His fame was on hiatus—indefinitely—thank you very much.

He set up his laptop on the kitchen table and pushed the power button. He'd work and avoid the television cameras. First, he jotted off a quick e-mail to send with his wireless modem.

Luke,
We're down to twelve already, so I might be home

sooner than you think. We've got two old couples (and one of the women, Millie, might commit murder by knitting needle to win), a pair of newlyweds and some people we knew in high school. It's been... interesting so far. Actually, very interesting.

He didn't say anything about Claire. Mark wasn't quite sure how he felt about her being here, but knew mentioning her to Luke would send him running over to see for himself. Instead, Mark added something about the Nova, then hit Send and switched to the file for the software manual he was working on.

If he could get the manual e-mailed out in the next couple days, he'd be one paycheck closer to his goal of helping Luke reestablish the business. Once he won the RV, he'd be able to sell it for enough to get their company off to a new start. Then he and Luke could get back to business in California and Mark would finally feel as if he had earned the partnership his brother had given him years ago. He'd never quite felt he'd deserved it and now, maybe, he could repay Luke for all that his brother had given him.

But it wasn't easy to work, not with the distraction of the TV crew. Renee was their current victim. "So, Miss Angelo, why do you want to win the RV?" The reporter leaned in with a smile.

"I want to win it for my grandpa, so he can retire and drive around the country." She looked sincere, but Mark remembered her mentioning a retiring grandma to Nancy.

The reporter asked her a few more questions about "Grandpa." Renee put on a woeful face, perhaps hoping to win pity from the viewing audience. Then he moved on to the others, asking them where they were from and why they wanted to win. Everyone repeated their reasons from this morning, some embellishing a bit to make a more dramatic case. Claire stood to one side, with the others who'd already been interviewed. Not even she'd managed to successfully dodge her shot at Hollywood.

Her face was still soft, tinged with sadness, her gaze on some faraway spot. He wondered where her thoughts had gone and what could possibly be so bad in Claire's life that she'd stand in the shower of a motor home and cry. The Claire he knew was stoic, optimistic. Never had he seen her upset or hurt, even when she'd fallen from the top of the monkey bars in third grade and skinned up her knees.

As a child, she'd been the Margaret to his Dennis the Menace. But as adults—

The very things that had driven him crazy were beginning to spark his interest. No, not just spark. Inflame.

He was still watching Claire when ten thousand watts, or maybe a hundred thousand, were thrust in his eyes. "James Kent." The reporter put out a hand and shook Mark's. "And you are?"

"Mark Dole."

The reporter, a slim young man with a slight tic in his left eye, flipped back a couple pages in his pad, to a series of notes about each of the contestants. "We got the list of contestants earlier from Nancy and did a little research," James explained, clearly eager to impress everyone with his journalistic skills. "Okay, you ready?"

"I'm working here." Mark gestured to the laptop.

"This will only take a second, I promise. Okay?"

Mark nodded, glancing at the pad uneasily again, then the light's full power hit his eyes, nearly blinding him.

"Mr. Dole, you've got quite the reputation in this town," James said into the mike, his voice now suddenly deep and serious, as if he'd hit puberty in the last five seconds. "Two-time all-star champ in both baseball and football, first place in the state track meet in your senior year, homecoming king in junior and senior year, voted most popular in your class."

"That was years ago," said Mark. The silent audience on the RV watched the exchange.

James consulted his pad again. "When you were ten, you rescued some boy caught on the ice, saved his—"

"Which has nothing to do with this."

"Oh, but it does. You're a hero, Mark Dole. Complete with the key to the city of Lawford to go with it." James slid the fuzzy black microphone under Mark's chin.

Heat rose up his neck, so thick it threatened to strangle him. "I'm not a hero. Just an ordinary guy."

"No." James let out a slight chuckle. "You're a story, my friend. Now, tell me about—"

"Find another story," Mark growled. He batted the mike away, got to his feet and stalked to the front of the RV.

Escape was impossible. Forty-five feet wasn't enough distance between him and the camera. Four million feet wouldn't have been enough, either. James followed doggedly behind, as if Mark held the secret to where Jimmy Hoffa was buried. Of all the questions in the world, Kent had to ask *that* one.

"You're the closest thing I have to a fairy tale," James said, in a soft, cajoling voice, the mike at his side so their conversation was off the record. "Small-town hero, superstar athlete, golden boy who could do no wrong. Heads off to California to make his way and fails—"

"How do you know about that?"

James snorted. "I'm a reporter. I make it my business to know. That's what makes this all so interesting. You were Achilles and something found your heel."

Mark refused to turn around. "Go torture someone else. I'm not interested in talking to you."

James leaned in close, his voice a whisper. "Frankly, most of the people on this overgrown bus are as interesting as fleas. What I need is a human angle, something to make the viewers tune in every day. Life's a soap opera, Mr. Dole, and the more we can exploit that, the higher our ratings."

Mark wheeled around. "You disgust me."

James shrugged. "That's what I get paid to do." He took the mike and tipped it toward Mark. "Now, are you going to tell me your side of the story?"

"No." Again, Mark pushed the microphone to one side, his hand cupping the foam head. "If you try to use any of this, I'll haul you into court so fast, you'll get whiplash."

The other man smiled a crafty smile and shook his head. "I don't think so. Remember that entry form you signed? Read the fine print, buddy. It said you agree to let the mall use your likeness, your story and practically your DNA to publicize this." He gestured to the cameraman, who flicked on the light again. "Now, let's pick up where we left off."

"I don't think so." Mark shoved past them, nearly toppling the cameraman, grabbed his laptop and headed back to the only private place in this hulking metal cage: the bathroom.

It took a single glimpse of Mark's face to know the reporter had pushed one button too many. Apparently James Kent agreed, because he didn't follow, just moved on to the next person. When Mark passed, Claire touched his arm. "You okay?"

She'd meant only to offer comfort, to check on a childhood friend. Nothing more. But a shock of electricity jolted her when she touched him, magnified when he turned and looked at her, his eyes now teeming oceans, dark as a storm. "No. I'm not."

"Want to talk?"

"Not especially."

She let go and reassumed her position against the kitchen counter, a safe distance from the energy steaming inside him. And, she had to admit, within her, too. It all felt so disconcerting, like standing on the edge of a cliff with a strong, pushy breeze at her back. "Okay."

He looked at her askance. "That's it? Just 'okay?'"

"Yeah. What'd you expect? Should I give you a ten-page questionnaire?"

Laughter bubbled up inside him and then escaped, like a teakettle releasing its steam. His features relaxed and his gaze lost some of its fierceness. "Most women wouldn't take no for an answer. They'd…well, pester me until I told them everything."

"In case you haven't noticed, I'm not most women." Claire made a sweeping gesture of her tall frame. "And I don't know who you're dating, but you might want to try someone with a little maturity under her belt."

He laughed again. "You surprise me."

"Glad to know I can still do that." A smile curved across her face.

"Remember the time in second grade when that fourth grader…what was his name? Oh yeah, Tommy Underhill. He was going to beat me up because I'd bumped into him at lunch and made him spill his pudding. I was a scrawny little runt then, but you, well, you seemed ten feet tall to the rest of us."

Claire toed at the vinyl floor. "Amazon, that's me."

"You stepped in there and told Tommy where to go

and what to take with him." Mark laughed and shook his head. "God only knows where you got that kind of vocabulary at eight."

"I had a colorful stepfather. He was a trucker." She let out a very unladylike snort. "When he bothered to work instead of lying on the couch and yelling at me to clean the house."

"Abe was your stepfather? But I thought—"

"Everybody thought he was my father. But he wasn't." She didn't elaborate.

Mark watched her for a moment, not saying a word.

Beside them, Millie and Lester had suspended their card game. They made little secret of their eavesdropping. Roger and Jessica were back on the couch, love-wrestling again. Danny had assumed his position in front of the television and was now joined by Tawny. John was just behind them, showing the photos of his kids to the television camera. Renee sat in the armchair, filing her nails. From the back bedroom, Claire could hear the sound of Art snoring and Gracie watching a soap opera.

"I didn't know that," he said quietly.

She traced the line between the squares on the floor. She turned a little so Millie would have to strain to hear. "Anyway, it's over now. Abe died a couple of months ago. He plowed his tractor trailer into a tree. Drinking and driving again."

"And your mother...she died when you were ten, right?"

Claire's boot left a thick black mark on the cream flooring, a temporary scar in the floral pattern. "Eleven." The word scraped by Claire's throat.

"Who raised you after that? Wasn't Abe gone a lot?"

Claire let out a gust of air. "You know, I asked you how *you* were doing. How did this end up being about me?" She shoved off from the counter and crossed to the sink, grabbing a plastic cup from the shelf and filling it with water. She clutched the drink and looked out the window at the shoppers and plastic plants. She refused to talk about the past. She intended to leave *all* of it behind in a few days. Dredging that mess up now would only complicate things. "What got you all riled up with that reporter?"

"Nothing."

She spun around. "Oh, I see. You want me to spill my whole life story, but when it comes to yours, you clam up." She took a sip and put the cup on the counter.

Mark glanced at the television crew. Claire's gaze followed. They now had Nancy framed in the entrance and were interviewing her against the backdrop of nosy shoppers. "They just got too personal."

"I know all about that." She nodded in the direction of Millie and Lester. Mark smiled. He gestured to her to follow. They went down the hall and ducked into the alcove created by the closet outside the bathroom.

"I'm sorry," he said.

"For what?"

"For getting too close with the questions. I hated it when it happened to me a minute ago. It's just…"

He didn't finish. He was looking at her in this odd way that could have been construed as *interest,* had he been anyone other than Mark. Only a few inches separated them and Claire was suddenly very aware of Mark, not as a friend, not as a competitor, but as a man.

"Listen, the air in here is doing weird things to all of us," she said. "Forget the whole thing."

His gaze narrowed, became more thoughtful. "Maybe we shouldn't."

"Shouldn't what?"

"Forget this happened. Maybe we should look at it as one step further along in our relationship."

She laughed. "Relationship? Mark, I know you. You don't have serious relationships. You're like a chain smoker who doesn't want to give up his three-pack-a-day habit, even if it kills him."

"You're saying I can't get serious about a woman?"

"Mark, when was the last time you committed to an aftershave, never mind a female? I've known you all my life. Face it—you've never been what anyone would consider marriage material." She cocked her head. "And you and I both know you're happier that way."

His face tightened, the storm resurged in his eyes. "I guess you know me pretty well," he said. "Maybe too well."

Then he walked away, headed for the kitchen. He settled into the dinette, flipped open his laptop and started typing like a madman. She got a book from her suitcase and tucked herself into a corner of the couch. She tried to concentrate on the thriller in her hands, but all her mind would focus on was Mark. On the dark passion in his eyes and the odd comment he'd just made.

Mark might as well have been sleeping on a bed of nails, for all the sleep he was getting tonight. He'd tucked his queen back into the pile, letting Art, who had a ten, and Gracie, who had a jack, take the bed over the cab. The bed he'd intended to share with Claire. Or maybe Tawny, or even Renee, who'd cornered him after dinner to tell him how handsome he'd gotten with age.

That's where he should be. Not here on this cold, hard floor, squeezed onto the thin strip of carpet between the two dinette benches, with an afghan Millie had knitted. The mall had planned ahead for everything but enough pillows and blankets. Undoubtedly, they'd expected more people to quit by now. But the twelve who were left had held on pretty well, at least for the first sixteen hours.

Especially Claire. He'd hardly been aware of anyone else, despite the crowded quarters. Ever since she'd pulled that stunt in the bathroom, he hadn't been able to put her from his mind. Whenever he tried to do anything—pour a glass of milk, eat a piece of the peach pie they'd had after dinner—he'd thought of nothing but the slip of soft skin she'd exposed, seemingly so much more bare beside the pastel blue of her bra.

The color was called peri-something, periwrinkle or peritinkle, he couldn't remember the name. But, oh, he could picture it all right. Every time he closed his eyes, he saw Claire's defiant eyes and saw the thin satin strap.

He'd never seen her in quite that light before and the discovery of her as a well-rounded, intelligent woman— not as the girl whose pigtails he'd pulled—was like stepping into virgin territory. Unfortunately, she'd clearly sealed off the borders. Claire was right about him. If there was one thing she was good at, it was getting right to the heart of the matter.

He was a hound. And he knew it. All his life, he'd chased women and caught virtually every one. When he was young, they'd wanted him because he'd had his picture in the paper, with the mayor of Lawford, no less, and for the teenaged girls of Mercy, that pretty much equaled stardom.

By the time he graduated high school, he'd perfected the art of charm. He knew how to hold a girl's coat while she put it on, just close enough to brush his fingers against her shoulder and then give her a slight, almost imperceptible squeeze. He knew to kiss her lightly on the first date, leaving her wanting more. He knew to wait a day to call after the date, to let her wonder if he'd keep his promise. He knew all those things and for the last fifteen years, he'd used them to his advantage. But with Claire...

Damn. With Claire, it was different. In the months since Luke's wife had died, Mark had started to look at women with new eyes. A psychologist might attribute it to that twin mentality, maybe Luke's sensibilities drifting over into Mark's mind. All Mark knew was that suddenly his twin's life had seemed so much more *complete* with a good woman and a steady home. Even though she was gone, Luke still had memories and videos and love letters—tangible proof of their love, which had extended much deeper than even Mark had realized.

He'd had a lifetime of dating women who were out for nothing more than a good time. Self-centered, unwilling to connect with anyone. Women who wanted him for his looks, and not much else. Claire was right. What he needed was someone with a little more maturity under her belt. Someone who had self-assurance and gumption in abundance.

Someone like Claire.

But trying to start anything at all with her was impossible. He couldn't rely on his old methods, the lines that used to sound so clever and now just sounded stupid. She'd see right through them, anyway. She had a way of looking at him, of seeing past the place where everyone else stopped. Of *knowing* him, predicting him, exposing him.

The thought of exposing anything at all got his pulse racing again. Sleep eluded him like a shadow on a gray day. He tossed off the afghan and got to his feet. He grabbed a beer out of the refrigerator, ripped off the cap and drank half of it before he let the door close.

The light spilled into the living area of the RV. In the

recliner, her feet tucked underneath her, was Claire. She had her head cradled in the crook of her arm, but she was awake. He saw the shimmer of light reflected in her eyes and wondered if she'd been watching him toss and turn. Had her thoughts been veering down the same dangerous road? Skidding like a car in a sudden snowstorm?

She sat up and the blanket puddled beneath her on the floor. Mark looked away—before the image of her Barbados nightshirt doing the same thing took up residence in his mind. She padded into the kitchen. "What are you doing up?"

"Couldn't sleep. They have more comfortable beds in the monkey cage at the zoo."

In the near-darkness, she was a softer version of Claire. Almost…vulnerable. She laughed quietly. "Any more beer left?"

He nodded and opened the door. The amber light from inside illuminated her face, making the hard edges and sarcasm he'd always associated with Claire seem to disappear. "Claire?"

"Hmm?" She reached into the fridge and extracted a bottle of light beer. She twisted off the cap, tossed it into the trash can, then took a drink. "What?"

"When this is over…"

"When I win, you mean." She tipped the bottle toward herself in emphasis.

"Maybe." He grinned. The tenacity of a bulldog, that was the Claire he knew. His heart accelerated. Was he nervous? He couldn't remember the last time he'd been worried a woman might turn him down. "When it's over, do you want to go out? On a date? With me?"

She was in the middle of her second sip when he asked the question. She started to choke, nearly spitting the beer back at him. "What did you say?"

"You. Me. Dinner. Maybe a movie. The first dance in the mating ritual." God, he wanted to slap his head. Why had he said that? It belonged in the book of world's worst pickup lines.

Claire laughed. "That's one I haven't heard before."

"That came out wrong." He wanted to kick himself. He stepped forward, took the beer from her hand and placed both bottles on the counter. "I'd…" he paused, realizing he actually *was* nervous, then tried again, "I'd like to take you out when this is over."

She blinked several times. The silence between them stretched for one second. Two. Three. "I don't think that's a good idea."

"Why not?"

"On our one and only date from hell, you dropped me off and peeled out of my driveway so fast, my stepfather planted a garden in the tire tracks."

"Come on, you're exaggerating."

"You didn't like me. I didn't like you."

"We were sixteen. We didn't know any better."

She shook her head. "I don't think anything's changed."

A tiny bit of light spilled in from the window, casting her in a subdued pattern of shadows and radiance. She smelled of vanilla, as delicious as homemade cookies. Without thinking, he reached up and touched her cheek. Beneath his palm, her skin was soft, smooth. Kissable. A fierce wave of desire slammed into him with tsunami force. He swallowed, acutely aware of the few inches separating them in the dark, intimate kitchen. "I think a lot's changed, Claire."

For the space of a heartbeat, she didn't move. She didn't even seem to breathe. Then she stepped back, broke the connection and the softness disappeared. "Have you?"

"Yes, I think I have. I've learned a lot this past year."

"And now you're suddenly thinking in terms of 'relationships?'"

"Maybe."

"Or maybe I'm that one banana on the tree you can't reach."

"That's not it. Claire—"

"Mark, why don't you start with a dog first? Get a puppy. Take care of it, feed it, pay attention to it every day. Try that on for a commitment before you make some woman promises you don't intend to keep."

His jaw hardened. To-the-point Claire had pinpointed all his flaws in one nice, neat paragraph. "Did someone do that to you?"

"Remember Leanne Hartford?"

He shook his head.

"Well, I do. And if you did, you'd understand why I don't trust you. Or many other men." She let out a sigh. "Either way, we're not talking about me." She grabbed her beer off the counter. "I suggest you get some sleep. You want to be well rested for your trip home tomorrow."

He'd blown it with that stupid line. He'd moved too fast, like some predatory hawk after a mouse. "I don't give up that easily, Claire."

"And I don't give *in* that easily." She turned and walked away. She didn't spare him a second glance as she crossed to her chair, plopped into it and covered herself with the blanket.

Who needs her anyway? There are plenty of women in the world. I don't need one who drives me crazy. Mark finished his beer, tossed the empty into the trash and went back to his spot on the floor. He tossed and turned, think-

ing over what she had said to him, realizing most of it
was quite close to the truth. Or at least the truth that used
to be his life, before he understood what Luke had lost
and realized how very much he wanted what his brother
had once had. The trouble was how to get it. How to
become a man who could be depended on to support his
family, to be there when things got rough.

Was he even that kind of man? He wasn't sure.

When Mark finally fell asleep, his dreams were washed
in peri-whatever blue.

"Day Two," Claire wrote in her journal.

The remaining twelve are plotting various methods
of murder. The space here is insanely cramped, making everyone ten times more annoying. And to top it
all off, there's only one bathroom to share with Art,
Gracie, Millie, Lester, Roger, Jessica, Renee, Danny,
John, Tawny…and Mark, though he's made it clear
he's more than happy to share. And what about me—
do I even want to go down that road with Mark?

Claire shut her journal before she answered that question, tucked the book into her bag and sighed. For half an
hour, she'd waited in the small hallway outside the bathroom, sitting on her suitcase and growing more and more
aggravated with Danny. The guy had come on board with
a paper bag for a suitcase, for Pete's sake, yet had managed to spend thirty minutes in the bathroom. She'd heard
him shower—singing a Sinatra tune while he did—then
run the faucet, then sing some more. He'd cycled through
a whole concert of Ol' Blue Eyes, but had yet to emerge.
She had no idea what could have kept him so occupied—
it had been ten minutes since she'd heard running water.

A few feet away, Millie was blending up some god-awful disgusting concoction in the kitchen. It smelled like fish oil and bran, all rolled into a green foamy beverage. Claire's appetite drained away.

Millie hit the pulse button and Claire felt the room start to topple. She leapt to her feet and banged on the door. "Danny! What'd you do? Die in there?"

"Out in a minute!" It was the same thing he'd said ten minutes ago. And fifteen minutes before that.

"Fifty-nine seconds," Claire called back. "Fifty-eight. Fifty-seven."

"Or what?"

"Or I come in there and haul you out by your briefs." She hammered on the door again. "Fifty-two. Fifty-one. Fifty."

"All right, all right." The door opened and Danny emerged, followed by a huge cloud of steam. "It's yours."

"Any hot water left?"

He shrugged and offered her a sheepish grin. "Sorry."

Claire bit her tongue, because what she wanted to say to him would probably set Millie's hair on fire, and dragged her suitcase into the bathroom.

Just before she shut the door, she caught a glimpse of Mark in the back bedroom. His laptop hummed beside him, but he wasn't using it. Instead, he was scribbling notes and numbers on a pad of paper. He added the column, shook his head, added it again, let out a curse.

Claire hesitated, caught quite literally in the doorway between a desperately-needed shower—not to mention a respite from the RV crowd—and Mark. She could see frustration in the sharp angle of his jaw, the tense set of his shoulders.

Last night, she'd had about five minutes of sleep. Every

time she closed her eyes, she saw Mark, felt his hand against her cheek, smelled the woods-fresh scent of his aftershave. In the space of less than twenty-four hours, he'd managed to push their friendship over a cliff and into territory she'd never imagined traversing with him. They were platonic friends from childhood, people who'd annoyed each other but stuck up for one another when the Tommy Underhills of the world got too close. Friends and nothing more, she reminded herself. Close quarters make people do crazy things.

She'd already given her heart to a guy like him. A man who'd convinced her living in a dumpy apartment in Mercy was the height of romance, then walked away when something better came along. She'd already had two men betray her bank account and her heart. She didn't need another one. Especially not when she was about to finally live her own life, not have her path dictated by someone with an overabundance of Y chromosomes.

She'd taken a half step into the bathroom when she heard Mark curse again. He tore off the top sheet from the pad and crumpled it into a ball. She could practically see the frustration emanating from him. Yesterday, he'd stepped in when Nancy would have refused her a place on the RV. Clearly, Mark could use someone to talk to. A few minutes of friendship wouldn't cost her anything. Would it?

She left her suitcase in the bathroom and went into the bedroom. "Need some help?"

He sat up with a jerk. His hair was a mess, as if he'd run his hands through it a hundred times. There were dark circles underneath his eyes and a day's worth of stubble on his chin. If she didn't know him better, she'd say Mark looked worried. "Claire. I didn't hear you come in."

"Millie's got the blender going," she said by way of

SHIRLEY JUMP   59

explanation. "It takes a lot of power to grind up all that fiber with the cod liver oil."

Mark made a face. "Are you serious?"

"That's what it smells like. I decided it was in my best interests to skip breakfast."

"Good choice." He glanced back at the pad.

"What are you working on?" The Mark she'd known before he'd moved to California five years ago didn't work on much more than getting a woman's phone number. But then again, this Mark didn't seem like the same man she remembered.

He snorted. "A miracle." He tossed the pad aside.

"Oh." She paused, leaving space for him to explain, but he didn't. "Next time, use your queen."

"Huh?"

"I saw you tuck your card back into the deck. You look like you could use a good night's sleep. Maybe a week of sleep." She took a seat on the corner of the bed. The mattress was firm. A pillow top, it felt like. Claire rolled her head, trying to work out the kinks in her neck. "Make sure you get a bed, though. That chair is made of concrete."

He laughed and slid across the bed. Before she could move or say no, his hands were on her neck, magical fingers massaging and kneading away a night's worth of discomfort. "Oh. *Oh.* That's nice." She swallowed. Heat radiated beneath his hands, traveling down her spine. "Very nice."

"You should have taken the bed I offered." His voice was low, dark. "Then we both could have had some sleep."

Claire jerked away and spun to face him. "Can't you go five minutes without trying to pick someone up?"

He scowled. "You think I was making a pass at you when I offered to share the bed above the cab?"

"Well, yeah. Since when are you into platonic relationships?"

"Since I met you in kindergarten." He shook his head. "Have I ever hugged you?"

"No."

"Kissed you?"

"No."

"Taken you in my arms and pledged my undying love?"

She laughed. "No, but you're welcome to try."

"Claire, you are my most successful and admittedly, maybe my only, platonic relationship with a woman." He brushed a stray hair out of her face and tucked it behind her ear. It was a simple gesture, not sexual in the least and yet… "That's not to say I haven't wanted to hug you. Or kiss you. Or lay you down on this bed and make love to you until neither one of us can think straight."

Heat rushed through her veins. Mark's hand was two inches from hers. His face, a few inches more. She was acutely aware of the firm mattress beneath her, of the images he'd created with his words. When had she started to think of Mark as anything other than a royal pain in the neck? When had he become a *man* in her eyes, not just a guy?

"Mark…" For once in her life, Claire was speechless. There was no witty rejoinder ready on her tongue. There was nothing in this room but a heightened awareness of the invisible, tensioning thread between them. It left her feeling vulnerable, out of step with herself.

"When I offered you a spot in the bed, I did it out of friendship. Last night, you made it very clear you don't feel what I feel." He gestured at her, then himself. "That this attraction between us—hell, that's not even a strong enough word for what I'm feeling—is one-sided.''

"Yeah, it is.'' And best to leave it that way, Claire thought. She was leaving this town for a new life, one that did not revolve around a man, particularly one whose idea of responsibility was making sure he shut the refrigerator door after drinking straight out of the milk carton. She cleared her throat and scooted off the bed. "I guess I still see you as the kid down the street.''

"I guess you do.'' He picked up the pad and pen again. "At least I'm always good for a back rub.''

She bit her lip and nodded, then fled the bedroom and all the implications that still hung in the air.

Just before she could grab the bathroom door handle, Lester brushed past her and hurried inside, moving surprisingly fast for a man who seemed to spend his life napping. He closed the door and set the lock.

"Hey! My suitcase is in there!'' Claire hammered on the door, but there was no response. She needed that shower ten times more now. At this point, she'd settle for a trickle of cold water and a toilet-paper towel. Anything to escape this RV, these people, Mark. "Let me in!''

"Don't bother him, dear.'' Millie laid a hand on Claire's arm. "Lester just drank his morning power shake. He'll be there awhile.'' Millie smiled, obviously knowing Lester's intestinal habits quite well. "A long while.''

Claire pressed a hand to her stomach, ignoring the images that little revelation conjured up, and glanced at Mark. He'd gone back to scribbling on the pad. His face held an intenseness she'd never seen before. The Mark she'd known had skated through school, barely lifting a pencil. Girls had practically prostrated themselves at his feet, offering to do his math or research his English paper.

The man on the bed wasn't the Mark she'd thought she

knew. And the woman who'd felt a charge of attraction when he'd brushed away a lock of her hair…that wasn't the Claire she knew, either.

The sooner she won this RV and headed for California, the better.

Chapter Four

Luke,

Thanks for picking up my car. Good news. It's early afternoon on Day Two and we're down two more. Tawny left for some party and John Madison (remember him from the football team?) left when his kids begged Daddy to come home. So far, it's going well. I spent most of the night on that manual I'm doing for Computer Solutions and I'm beat. Off to get a shower, if there's any hot water left.

Mark signed off, shut down the laptop, then stood outside the bathroom and waited for whoever was inside to emerge. After a night of work and tinkering with another idea that hadn't quite gelled yet, he was frustrated, tired and cranky. And in desperate need of a shower.

Finally, Art emerged and shuffled out into the kitchen. "All yours, buddy."

"Thank you." Mark headed inside, his gym bag slung

over his shoulder. He turned on the shower, then dug in his bag for toiletries. His hands came across clothes, underwear, deodorant, socks, a toothbrush, a metal tin of cookies and an electric razor. And that was it.

No soap. No toothpaste. No shampoo. He thought of Claire's suitcase and how he'd kidded her about bringing too much. Ginger had always managed to look good on *Gilligan's Island.* He suspected that had less to do with her superior packing skills and more to do with a great makeup crew behind the scenes. Claire's words came back to haunt him. He was about as unprepared as a man could get. At least he'd brought clean underwear. His mother would be proud. Tucking his ego into the bag along with his sweats, Mark turned off the water and headed out to find Claire.

She was seated at the dinette, playing euchre with Gracie, Art and Millie. Lester was stretched out on the couch, hock-hock-hocking away again.

"Claire, I need a favor."

She thumbed through her cards, selected a king of hearts and tossed it into the center of the table. "Hmm?"

He leaned down to whisper in her ear. "I, ah…forgot to bring soap." He paused. "And toothpaste." Paused again. "And shampoo."

Claire folded her cards into a pile and laid them face down on the table. She took her time turning to face him. When she did, she wore a smirk of huge proportions. "Really? So, Gilligan, you admit you underpacked?"

"A little."

"Or is it possible you underestimated the competition and didn't bring enough to sustain you?"

He wasn't admitting to anything. "Maybe."

She picked up her cards again and fanned them out.

Play had come around to her and she tossed out a ten of spades. "That's trump," she said to the others.

"So, can I borrow some of your stuff?"

"You're the enemy, Mark. Wouldn't that be like handing out hot meals to the British during the Revolution?"

"I wouldn't call it that."

"If I let you suffer, maybe you'll give up quicker." She grinned, then scooped up the trick she'd won and placed it beside her.

She had a point. Why should Claire help him? She wanted the RV as badly as he. Well, maybe not that much. But she was one determined woman, and if she set out to win, she'd hold on to the very last second. But so would he.

He watched her lead with trump and realized he held a trump card of his own. "I have something you want. Interested in a trade?"

She scooped up another trick, then led with an ace. From his vantage point above her, he could see the tip of her bra beneath the bright turquoise V-neck she wore. Black, just as she'd promised. "What could *you* have that I would want?"

"A full tin of my mother's homemade chocolate chip cookies."

She turned to face him. "Your mother packed you cookies?" Her voice was edged with laughter.

"Hey, my mother loves me. What can I say? She thought I might get hungry."

Claire probably wasn't aware she had licked her lips. When they were kids, his mother had often handed out little baggies of cookies to the neighbors. Claire was very familiar with Grace Dole's superior baking abilities.

"Are they the soft ones she makes at Christmas? With the walnuts?"

"Yep. And I have about three dozen in my bag."

"Instead of toothpaste, soap and shampoo."

He raised his hands in surrender. "I'm a guy. I thought of my stomach first."

"Claire!" Gracie, her partner in the game, called in irritation. "It's your turn."

Claire chose a card from the two in her hand and tossed it at the table. "Sorry. I don't need any cookies." The growling from her stomach belied her statement.

"Why? Did you fill up on power shakes this morning?" he whispered.

She grimaced and shuddered a bit. "Okay. How many cookies will you give me?"

"One for each item. Since I plan on being here awhile, that would mean three cookies. Every day. And if I'm feeling especially grubby, sometimes twice a day. Right after breakfast. Unless you'd rather have a shake?"

She considered his offer. The light in her eyes danced and a playful smile tickled at the edges of her mouth. "You have a deal." She stuck out a hand.

When he took her hand in his own, a charge detonated in his veins. Long, thin fingers, graceful yet strong. He was tempted to take her palm and kiss it, just to inhale the vanilla scent of her. He had no idea what the name of her fragrance was, but knew he'd never forget it. But instead of doing what he really wanted to do, Mark dutifully shook her hand and let go.

"Claire! Are you playing this game or not?"

"Oh, sorry." Claire spun around. A flush crept up her cheeks. Her ponytail swung from side to side.

Mark took that as one hell of a good sign. Maybe she was more interested in him than she wanted to admit. Her hand trembled a bit as she laid her last card on the table. She won the trick, but barely seemed to notice. Art scooped up the cards and began to shuffle. Claire pushed back from the table and got to her feet. ''I'll be right back.''

''You can't walk away in the middle,'' Millie protested.

''I'll be right back,'' she repeated.

Mark followed her down to the bedroom. She hefted her suitcase onto the bed and opened it. He supposed he should avert his eyes. But the momentary look she'd given him yesterday at what she wore beneath her tank had piqued his curiosity, as had the all-too short preview he'd had a moment ago.

Before he could get a clear glimpse of anything besides denim, she'd hauled out a plastic zippered bag and handed it to him. Curse Claire for being so organized. He would have rather seen her dump out her suitcase so he could see exactly what color indigo was.

''Need anything else?''

''No, thanks.'' Mark tucked the bag under his arm and headed back to the bathroom.

While he showered, every bubble of vanilla-scented lather reminded him of Claire. The fragrance was not too feminine, for which he was thankful. Nevertheless, it overpowered his mind, took him down paths he shouldn't go.

He imagined the same bar slipping along Claire's skin, its clean, light scent gracing her body, foaming under the hot water. He closed his eyes, picturing her naked skin glistening with water, flushed with heat—

''Hey, man, I need to get in there,'' Danny whined from the other side of the door. ''Those beans I had are done in my stomach. Way done.'' He groaned, let out a belch. ''Come *on,* man.''

The water might as well have turned to ice. Mark sighed and shut it off. When Danny let out another urgent

groan, the last vestiges of Mark's illicit daydreams about
Claire got sucked down the drain with the soapy water.

After Mark borrowed her soap and shampoo, Claire had
given up trying to play cards. She'd given her seat to
Renee, who annoyed the other players with so many how-
to-play questions that they'd disbanded a few minutes
later. Now everyone was watching television, ignoring
each other quite well.

Claire leaned against the refrigerator, ostensibly sipping
a soda. Her gaze strayed to the bathroom more than once.
More than a hundred times. Imagining Mark lathering
with her shampoo, the suds dripping down his arms, along
his shoulders...

Claire shook herself. What was she doing? Picturing
Mark naked? Those kinds of thoughts led straight down
Trouble Lane.

She'd been down that particular road already. She could
give directions, for Pete's sake. Nope, no more of that.
Claire was older. Wiser. Not falling for a man because he
had a good smile. And a lean build. And hands that could
handle a woman as easily as a wrench.

T-R-O-U-B-L-E, her mind sang. But even as it did, she
wondered if Mark wouldn't be trouble, if he'd be something so much more.

Crazy thoughts. Claire jerked away from the refrigerator and sat down at the kitchen table. She grabbed the
cards and dealt out a game of solitaire. There. She'd concentrate on cards. She was stronger than her hormones.

Yeah, right.

Danny passed by, clutching his stomach and groaning.
He began banging on the bathroom door and shouting
to Mark.

Her cell phone rang. She scrambled to pull it out of her back pocket and flip it open. "Dad?"

"Hi, honey. Thought I'd call and see how you were."

Even though the cell was an expense she couldn't afford, she was glad she had it. She would have gone crazy on the RV, not knowing how her father was doing. "I should be asking you."

"I'm just fine. Better now than this morning. I thought I'd—" he stopped, let out a few coughs, "let you know I was okay. Didn't want you to worry."

She clutched the phone and closed her eyes. "Thanks."

"You know, I don't think I told you this before, but…" his voice trailed off.

"What?"

"I'm really glad you tracked me down. It was a big surprise to find out I had a child. I know it took me a little while when you first contacted me and I'm sorry about that." He paused, cleared his throat. "I just never imagined I'd have kids and now…well, I'm glad you came along when you did."

"I'm glad I found you, too, Dad." Claire cradled the phone to her ear. He was her only family. She couldn't lose him before she got to know him. "I'll be out there soon to meet you," she said softly, then they ended the call.

Claire had essentially been an orphan until she'd found her father. But without a way to traverse the country, she had nothing more than a phone to connect them. A plane ticket bought a temporary visit. Claire wanted—*needed*— a lifelong change.

She'd blown nearly all of her savings and maxed out her credit card on a private investigator, but it had been worth it. For too long, Claire had been alone. Her mother, an only child, had died when Claire was eleven, three months after her mom's own parents had died. For the rest of her childhood, there'd been no grandparents. No aunts or uncles. No cousins. No brothers. No sisters. Abe Richards had been useless as any kind of family member. His only job had been to graciously drain her inheritance. Mom had left him the house, maybe thinking if he owned it, he'd give Claire a roof over her head.

Instead, he'd heavily mortgaged it, wasting the money on alcohol and bad football bets. She'd always thought she could count on the house, but when Abe had died in June and left her the house—and the high second mortgage—she was forced to sell it to pay off his debts, using her savings to pay the rest. All that had been left were a few boxes and a worn, smelly couch.

She hadn't told her father, or anyone, that the RV was her only hope. Her car wouldn't make a cross-country trek. After settling Abe's debts, she had even less money than before. She needed every penny she had to fund her new life and move her belongings. She could stay at an RV campsite until she found a job and a place to live. She had enough saved for security, first and last month's rent on a new place, plus a car hauler for the RV, but not much more.

Failure was not an option, Claire reminded herself. Again, the thought nagged at her that maybe this RV competition wasn't such a good idea. What if it didn't work out? What if she failed?

And worse…what if she wasn't as ready for a change as she thought?

The canned air of the RV must be doing things to her thinking, she decided. Claire tucked the phone into her jeans and glanced around the room. The others sat in front of the television like immovable stone statues.

Somehow, she'd get them all to leave. Even if she had to resort to desperate measures.

Luke,

When you come by next time, bring some of Mom's peanut butter cookies, please. I've found her cookies are a very nice bribe for bathroom time.

It's Day Five now and the tension in here is so thick, you could touch it. I've spent most of my time on the manuals. I got one done and started a second. The thought of doing another one bores me already, but I need the job.

See you later today. Don't forget the cookies!

Mark

He thought about asking Luke to bring him shower supplies, but decided for now it was far more fun to borrow from Claire. He signed off, sent the e-mail and reluctantly began work on the next manual. He'd amassed a couple thousand dollars in the last few weeks, but he needed more. Much more. With the sale of the RV, he'd have enough to fund a new start for their business. Maybe then he could get Luke back at work and give them both something to focus on besides the past. And he might finally feel like he was accomplishing something worthwhile with his life. Making a difference, doing something that had meaning and resonance—the way Luke always had.

The business had been Luke's idea, one that Mark had enthusiastically supported. They'd always done everything together—high school, college, prom dates. And so, when Luke had offered him a position, Mark had gladly accepted it. He hadn't yet found his niche in life, his mission, the spark that would make him roll out of bed in the morning, anxious to face the day, to reach that star on his own. So when Luke offered him the position, he'd gladly accepted.

And then he'd messed it all up. Blown an account, lost the business. Rectifying that mistake was his top goal right now. After that, who knew?

Claire's face came to mind and he wondered if he could convince her that he had changed, too. That he was *still* changing, finding himself and his place in life.

In the background, he heard the beginning of an RV riot. It was, after all, approaching the time for *The Young and the Rich* or whatever that soap opera was called. Every day, the women girded up for the TV control battle. Today, Millie was threatening Danny with bodily harm if he didn't hand over the remote at one o'clock.

Claire came up and took the seat beside him at the banquette. "It's getting ugly, isn't it?"

Ever since the first day, putting Claire from his mind had been impossible. Everywhere he turned, every thought he had, came back to Claire. Being around her had forced him to reexamine a few things about himself. Things he'd successfully ignored for nearly twenty years, and now...

Well, now he wasn't content with that status quo. Skating through life didn't give him the satisfaction of knowing whether he could actually achieve anything himself. Having things handed to him on a plate because he was Mark Dole, a name that still resonated something about heroism to people, had begun to make him feel like a fraud.

And that was the very thing Claire accused him of being. She wasn't, as she'd said, the one banana on the tree he couldn't reach. No, it was much more. She was the first person in his life he wanted to impress, wanted to show he was more than a name and a reputation.

Everyone had always labeled Luke the responsible one, the overachiever who worked hard for his grades, his business, his family. When they'd been kids, every one of Luke's achievements had been celebrated with cake and chocolate milk. If they hadn't been mirror images of each other, no one would have known Luke and Mark were twins.

Mark had won soccer games, thrown touchdown passes, had even held the two-hundred-meter record for three years at Mercy High. But things that required brains and thinking were not where he'd been praised. He was too old to be the football hero anymore. But he wasn't sure he had it in him to be a hero of anything else.

"Maybe we need to ask Nancy for a second satellite dish," Claire said.

"That's not in our best interests," he said, glad to talk about something else. "You start eliminating the things people fight over and there's even more incentive for them to stay."

"I don't know about that theory. No one seems ready to leave right now."

Claire turned to look at the crowd in the living room. Mark had a clear view of the curve of her neck, exposed by her ponytail. A long, graceful neck, giving her an almost regal bearing. If he pressed his lips against that skin, it would be soft, tender. If she sighed, the vibration of her voice would flutter against his lips, fanning the flames roaring in his gut. "Sometimes fighting makes people more attracted rather than less."

"Sometimes," she said quietly, then seemed to catch herself in the vulnerable moment. She turned back, her face shifting into a sour look. "I want them all to leave. As soon as possible."

"And then what?"

"And then I take this RV to California and start my life."

"You're moving?"

"Absolutely. I should have gotten out of this town ten years ago but I didn't. Now look at me. My career up to now has been putting pink rollers in gray hair. When I was eighteen, I had dreams, hopes—" she cut off the words and bit her lip. "Then I threw them away for some stupid guy and ended up stuck in Mercy."

Claire rose and headed to the refrigerator. He wanted to ask her who had made her so bitter, what guy could possibly have talked Claire into anything. She'd always seemed so headstrong to him, so in control.

Maybe Claire wasn't juggling all the balls of life as well as he'd thought. Maybe she knew what it felt like to be hemmed in by your past until escaping it became a Herculean effort.

She handed him a soda. "Thanks." He popped the top and sipped, unable to stop watching her. She made everything seem like an act of grace. Of something uniquely Claire.

"What happened to make you swear off guys?"

"Since when are you interested in my life?"

"Since you came back into mine."

She shook her head. "I'm not *in* your life, Mark. I'm just in the same RV as you." She took a seat at the table, grabbing her book. "I'm not looking for a relationship. I'm not even sure I'm ready for one. Not now. Not when I have—" She cut herself off. "Well, other things to deal with." And then she began to read, effectively shutting him out.

Well, that went well. Mark took his soda and headed into the living room. At the door, he saw two familiar faces peeking in. Luke and Emily. After days of strangers and neighbors gawking at the windows, his twin and niece were a welcome sight.

Mark opened the door and took a seat, tucking himself into the doorway so his position couldn't be construed as stepping outside the vehicle. A circle of people formed around the RV, craning their necks to peek inside but probably couldn't see past him. The crowd dispersed a moment later. "Hey, lesser of two evils, how are ya?"

The nickname people had given Luke, the better behaved of the twins, brought a smile to his brother's face. "Okay." But the dark shadows beneath his eyes and his painfully gaunt body belied the words. Luke was not okay. He hadn't been since his wife died more than a year ago.

Eleven-year-old Emily scuffed at the mall floor, looking more bored than anyone on the planet. She held a shopping bag from one of the teen stores in the mall. "Hey, Uncle Mark."

"Hey yourself, goose."

She rolled her eyes at the nickname, but he caught a hint of a smile playing at her lips.

"So tell me the truth." Luke gestured at the RV and handed over the tin of peanut butter cookies in his hand. Mark could see Luke make an effort at banter. "You in there with the Notre Dame cheerleading squad or what?"

"Better."

Luke hesitated until Emily wandered over to a sidewalk sale display. "Better than perky females in short skirts who really dig athletic guys?"

"I haven't been considered athletic for a while. Too much time in an office for that." As soon as the words were out, Mark wanted to take them back. The office was no more. Gone. Reminding Luke of that was cruel. Damn, he felt like a jerk. So he did what any jerk did—barreled on and hoped the comment went unnoticed. "Anyway, there's a few people in here I could do without, but there's one who's made it almost...fun."

Luke raised an eyebrow. "Fun as in trying out the bed in the back or fun as in playing Parcheesi?"

"Fun as in Claire Richards."

"Claire? The Amazon?"

Even though the words had come from Luke, and were not meant to be offensive, they sparked a flare of defensiveness in Mark. "Hey, she's elegant."

Luke chuckled. "Sounds like she's become more than just the girl down the street to you."

Mark shrugged. "Maybe."

"Since when do you get serious about a woman?"

Even his own twin saw him as a playboy. If Luke couldn't see past that high-school image, would anyone else ever be able to? "I'm twenty-nine. It's time I grew up."

Luke nodded. "You need a woman who will keep you in line. Mary used to—" he cut the words off abruptly.

Mark could almost feel the razor-sharp edge of Luke's grief. There were so many things Mark wanted to say to Luke, but he didn't know where to begin. "I'm sorry" would be a start, but how did a man begin to apologize for losing the biggest account of their business and essentially flushing the entire operation down the toilet, at the very time when Luke needed him most?

How did he begin to atone for that? For leaving Luke and Emily, and himself, with no other option than to return to Mercy, tails tucked between their legs, and move in with their parents, like flunking college students?

Mark rubbed a hand over his face and didn't say a word. He had to win this damned RV. Immediately. Then he could drive it to California, sell it to the highest bidder, and fund another start for both of them, proving himself in his own eyes, and in those of the people who'd never seen him any other way.

"Speaking of grown-ups, Katie had her babies, one of each. We're uncles again, as of midnight."

"She did? That's great! She looked ready to pop when she and Matt came over for Sunday dinner last week. Geez, they didn't waste much time. They only got married a year ago." The sight of his baby sister, grown up and starting a family of her own, had only intensified the longing Mark had been feeling lately for the very same thing.

"She says she saw you on the news last night and it sent her into labor." Luke chuckled. "I didn't know this was going to be on TV."

"Yeah, there's this annoying reporter skulking around all the time. I hope he won't be back for a while."

"Well, I'd best get going," Luke said. "Emily got a check from the folks for some back-to-school clothes and she's intent on blowing it as quickly as possible." He glanced over at her. She had her hands filled with shirts and jeans. "Guess it won't take long."

Mark laughed. "Hey, thanks for coming by."

Luke nodded. "Good luck on winning this thing. While you're here, you should work on that training program you were always talking about. You know, the one that turns the Greek I write into English?"

In between manuals, Mark had started working on that plan, but it refused to take shape. He wasn't sure he could make it work. Thus far, all he'd come up with was some gibberish for an idea that hadn't quite gelled into anything workable. "I don't know, Luke. That was just an idea. I was talking out of my hat."

"It was a *good* idea. You have a way with people that I don't have. You can explain things without making them feel stupid. I know you're writing manuals, but that idea for a program and classes…it's great.'' Luke rubbed his chin. ''You know, when you proposed the idea, I didn't think it would work. But with the right teacher…''

''Who?''

''You.'' Luke let out a laugh. ''Yeah, I know. I see that look on your face. Just think about it, will you? If I wrote the computer babble and you helped translate it to people, I think we'd have a hit on our hands.''

''Maybe.''

''Definitely.'' Luke glanced at Emily, then back at Mark. ''Oh, if you need to be picked up, you might want to ask Dad.'' Luke ran a hand down the side of the doorway, avoiding Mark's gaze. ''I took a job at the steel mill.''

Mark sighed. ''Luke, you can do better.''

''I have a daughter to support. Technology jobs aren't exactly growing on the cornstalks in Indiana. I'm not picky—I just need to make a living.'' Luke shrugged as if he didn't care, but Mark knew better. His twin had an amazing, intricate mind that could create lines of code worthy of a Nobel Peace Prize. And now, instead of scrolling a mouse, Luke was hefting steel.

Because of you. Because you let down your brother and the business at exactly the wrong time.

Mark thanked his brother for the cookies and promised to keep him updated by e-mail. Luke gave a wave and walked over to join Emily. There was a slump in Luke's shoulders, caused by a sadness that hadn't been there a year ago. Mark wished all over again that he had the power to lift that burden. If only—

''You look like you need a jalapeño popper.'' Claire took a seat beside him and held out a plate filled with breaded, cheese-stuffed appetizers. She even had a tiny tub of raspberry sauce to go with them. "Plus, I wanted to apologize for being short with you earlier. I overreacted. And…" she paused, her face softening, becoming a different Claire than the one he normally saw, "I'm sorry."

"This is a great apology." He welcomed the respite. If his thoughts were fists, he'd have beaten himself to a pulp a long time ago. "Where'd you get these?"

"Did you think I only had clothes in my suitcase?" She laughed, dipped one breaded ball in sauce, popped it into her mouth, munched for a second. She'd let her hair down and the soft blond waves curled over her shoulders, framed her face. She'd also changed into a snug white V-necked T-shirt, emblazoned with Women Rule in bright-pink sparkly letters. "I'm a snack junkie. I brought everything but your mother's homemade cookies." She pointed at him. "Speaking of which, you owe me three for today."

"They'll be in your hands soon as I'm done with these." Though he averted his eyes and blocked the image of her golden hair from his mind, his thoughts kept coming back to her. Wondering why she was here, why she'd thought of his stomach, why she kept coming around—a friend when he needed one most. But whenever he tried to get close to her, she pulled away. Push. Pull. Was she interested? Or pitying him? And how would she feel when he won the RV and drove away?

And why was he suddenly so driven to get close to her, to know her better? To pursue something more solid than a date or two?

Mark selected a plump popper, dipped it and tossed it into his mouth. "You really know the way to a man's heart."

She laughed and took another one. A comfortable silence formed between them, born from years of knowing each other.

"I remember the first time I met you," Mark said, his mind reaching back decades, pulling the images into the present. "You were five, I think. Yeah, five. I know, because I distinctly remember turning six the day before. You were riding your bike for the first time without training wheels. I was so damned jealous. I hadn't mastered my two-wheeler yet and here you were, a *girl,* zipping down the street in front of my house. You stopped at the end of my driveway, just to show off, I think."

"I remember that," Claire said. She shook her head and let out a soft chuckle. "God, that was ages ago. That was the first time we met? I thought it was the time I pushed you into Jimmy Brown's wading pool."

"Nope. That was our second introduction. It's amazing we talk to each other today, after all that." He bit off the end of a popper and got nothing but jalapeño. His eyes watered. "When you rode by, I hated you for doing something I couldn't." He laughed. "You know how six-year-old boys are. The whole world revolves around themselves."

Claire raised an eyebrow. "And when exactly do men outgrow that thinking?"

Mark grinned. "For some of us, never."

"That's what I thought." She dipped another, swirling the breaded concoction in the raspberry sauce, then put it in her mouth. A drop of cranberry-colored sauce lingered at the corner of her mouth.

Sweet. Hot. Edible. He could lean forward, with the least amount of effort, and lick that droplet of raspberry off her lips. With nothing more than a half an inch of movement, he could capture her mouth—that bright-red, please-kiss-me mouth—take her with his, taste the sweetness and heat that was Claire.

Before he could act on what every inch of his body was screaming at him to do, she produced a napkin and wiped away the sauce. Damn.

"These are really good," he said, meaning everything but the poppers.

"Thanks." She held one up, looking at it before taking a bite. "I make them myself. It's kind of a hobby, you know—cooking. I used to think I'd grow up and become a chef, but I didn't." She laughed. "My kitchen is filled with cookbooks and appliances and special bowls and—"

"Claire." He heard the insistence in his voice. She started, and he knew she heard it, too.

"Wh-what?"

"I want to—" he cut himself off. He might want to do a million different things with her, some here in the little corner of privacy they'd created, many more things in the RV's bedroom. But that wasn't the reason he'd come. It wasn't the motive behind staying until Millie and Lester and Art and Gracie and all of them gave up and went home.

Mark looked away, down the long tiled corridor of the mall. Luke. Emily. The business. *That* was what he needed to focus on. For once, Mark needed to think about something besides his own needs. Claire would be there later. "I want to…get those cookies now, before I forget."

"Oh." A flicker of disappointment shone in her eyes. "Sure. That would be great." She hoisted another popper in her hand. "The perfect antidote to these."

Mark swallowed. "Yeah. Something like that."

Chapter Five

Day Six. I've spent three nights in the chair and two on the floor, because I keep drawing low cards. My back and legs are aching constantly and I'm about ready to share a mattress with the Hunchback of Notre Dame if it means a real bed instead of a chair. I've played a thousand games of solitaire, but it's not helping keep my mind off my dad and winning this RV.

And Mark. Mark is so different from what I remembered. He's still attractive, of course, but now, he's a little more…mature, I guess. Is it possible he's starting to leave that playboy attitude behind? He says so, but I'm not so sure—

"Here's my payment for today." Claire shut her journal at the sound of Mark's voice. He laid three chocolate chip cookies before her. "Luke came by again and replenished my supply."

Claire had always liked Mark's twin, a gentle, serious guy who could usually be found with his nose in a book. She'd read about the death of Luke's wife last year in the paper and couldn't imagine how difficult it must be for him to raise his daughter alone. But Emily was lucky. Even though she'd lost her mother, she still had a father who cared, and grandparents to try to fill the void. "How is Luke doing?"

Mark settled into the seat across from her. "Surviving."

"It must be hard."

"Impossible." He shook his head. "They'd been married since they were seventeen." Mark fiddled with a cookie. "I think half the time he only gets up in the morning because he has to."

"For Emily."

"Yeah. If it weren't for her, I don't know where he'd be. Where any of us would be, for that matter. It's a lot easier to focus on the problems of an eleven-year-old girl than on the empty place at the table."

"I know what you mean. My mother died when I was the same age as Emily. It's been almost twenty years, but there are still days when I miss the sound of her voice or wish I could talk to her." Claire shook her head.

He leaned forward. "Is that why you never get close to anyone?"

Claire shifted to put some distance between them. The space was warm, even with the cooling system blowing. "I get close."

He arched an eyebrow. "Name one person you're close to."

"Jenny. Remember her? She used to date your brother Nate. She lives next door to me."

"I do. I also remember she was the best thing for my

younger brother, too." A lock of hair fell in his eyes and he reached to brush it away. Before he could, Claire's hand automatically went to the spot. Their fingers connected and a jolt of electricity coursed through her.

"I'm…I'm sorry," she stammered, surprised at herself. Claire Richards never stammered. Never lost her cool. Never let the touch of a man—a friend—drive her to distraction. "I was just…" She didn't finish.

Mark captured her hand before she could retreat. "Don't."

"Don't what?"

"Pull away. We're just talking. Like friends."

She swallowed. "You're holding my hand. That's more than friends."

"Only if you feel more than friendly feelings for me." He paused for a heartbeat. "Do you?"

The lock of hair stubbornly fell across his brows again. "You need a haircut," Claire said. She got to her feet, tugging her hand away. "I…ah, have my scissors with me. You know me, overpacking queen." Her laughter was forced. "Anyway, I could do it now. If you wanted."

Anything to get out of this conversation. Away from this cramped, too-hot kitchen where nothing seemed to exist but Mark.

He studied her for a long second, his gaze taking in her full height towering above him. Then he got to his feet. "Sure. I trust you."

She couldn't resist a grin. "Are you sure? In high school, you seemed more worried about your appearance than your next meal," she teased.

"I've changed. Grown up." He took a step closer, invading her space again. "Haven't you noticed?"

Oh yeah, she had noticed. More than once since they'd boarded the RV together. She'd noticed when he'd brushed by her, the scent of male and woods tempting her nostrils. She'd noticed when he'd stood and stretched after breakfast, all lean muscle and V-shaped man. She'd noticed *everything*.

The haircut offer had been a bad idea. She'd cut hundreds of people's hair, but never had her job seemed like such an intimate act before. Almost like kissing...only closer.

This was a very bad idea. Then why did she suddenly feel a twinge of anticipation?

Mark settled himself into one of the fold-up barstools in the kitchen, the only chair high enough to match Claire's height. Claire had spread yesterday's newspaper over the carpet and clipped a towel firmly around his neck with some plastic vise thing she called a "claw." She'd pulled her own hair back into a ponytail and now stood over him, scissors in one hand, straight comb in another.

He wondered about her withdrawal earlier. Was he that repulsive? Or was she so interested that his nearness had scared her? He wanted to ask her again why she kept resisting him, why she'd clearly sworn off men, why...

Why he didn't seem to stand a chance with her. And why it mattered so damned much that he did.

"Ready?" she asked.

"I did tell you I trusted you, right?"

She grinned. "You sure did."

"Now don't go cutting my hair into some bowl shape—"

"Shut up, Mark." But her voice was soft, undemanding. Her fingers ran through his hair, measuring, analyzing. Or at least that's what he told himself she was doing. All the while, he kept thinking how the touch of her hands felt like heaven.

"You have nice hair," she said. Was it his imagination or was her voice husky?

"I don't think anyone's ever said that to me before." He tipped his head to grin at her. "Most women compliment other parts of me."

Her gaze narrowed. "I'm only concerned with your head. Now sit still."

Dutifully, he lowered his chin. The comb slid into his hair. Claire lifted a section and snip...the ends floated to the floor. Comb, lift, snip. Again and again, she repeated the process, working her way through his hair. Her touch was light, feminine. Professional and not the least bit sexy. But in this setting, with her body so close to his, every whisper of the scissors, every touch of her hand, scorched him like fire.

"Why aren't you married?" he asked.

Her hand stilled. "Mark, this is neither the time nor the place—"

"It's a simple question, Claire. One everyone asks at high-school reunions. You're a beautiful woman. You're smart, you're funny. You wear indigo." A small grin crossed her face. "Why hasn't some lucky guy snatched you up?"

She bent forward and started cutting again, but this time the movements seemed stiffer, less fluid. "There are no eligible males under the age of ninety in Mercy."

"Sure there are. There's me, for one."

"Maybe I should have qualified that. Eligible *marriage-material* males."

"You don't think I'm marriage material?"

She laughed so hard the scissors shook. Millie looked up from her knitting; Roger and Jessica peeked up from their snuggling on the couch; Art and Gracie paused in their newspaper reading; Renee shot them a look of annoyance from her seat by the TV. Even Danny turned around to see what was so funny. Lester, however, kept on napping.

"Hey, hey, careful with those things!" Mark said.

"Oops, sorry." Claire stifled her laughter and brought the scissors back under control.

"I take that as an insult. I'm not *that* bad."

Claire moved and cut, murmuring an agreement Mark was sure she didn't mean. She finished the back of his head and came around to the front. She slipped into the space between his legs, humming a bit to herself as she trimmed. She was closer than any professional hairdresser had ever been. On purpose?

He'd had his hair cut plenty of times but never had he been more aware of the person doing the cutting. Claire's hips curved graciously into the space allowed by his legs. If she moved a half an inch to either side, she'd be pressed against his inner thigh. He alternately wished Claire would move away—and while she was at it, douse him with cold water—and that she would press against him and bring relief to the agonizing torture of not touching her.

He cleared his throat. "So…why didn't you ever settle down with one guy?"

"I haven't met one who cared to settle down. As Miss Marchand, one of my customers, would say, I must have Use Me stamped on my forehead."

Mark leaned back, a look of surprise on his face. "You? You've always been so…forceful."

She snorted. "No. I'm a sucker for a good line." Claire directed his head back into position. "Or at least I used to be. I was quite the loser magnet when I was younger."

"You're a magnet for any man."

"Yeah, especially men who have no intention of hanging around." She lifted another section of hair. "Anyway, I'm cutting your hair right now. Not talking about me."

He reached out and grasped her waist, lifting his gaze to hers. She pulled her hands back, comb and scissors in midair. Most likely everyone on the RV was watching, but Mark didn't care. "Is it the men who don't want to hang around? Or you? Why are you really leaving Mercy, Claire?"

She looked at him, eyes wide, lips parted, as if she were about to tell him something, to open her heart and let him in. But then a series of sharp raps sounded at the front door. "I'll get it," Claire shouted. She broke out of his grasp and dashed for the front door, scissors and comb still in her hands.

Through the glass, Claire could see the two ladies standing outside the RV. The Misses, as they were called in town. Miss Marchand, the toughest biology teacher ever to reign at Mercy High, and Miss Tanner, her irascible neighbor. They were two of Claire's regular customers. Every Saturday at ten—a wash and set. Always the same pink rollers, followed by a twenty-minute stay under the dryers where they caught up on back issues of *People* magazine and shouted gossip to each other.

Saved by the bell, Claire thought. Mark's questions had hit on all the things she didn't want to think about—her past, her future and her relationships with men. Why did he suddenly care so much? And why did that attention make her feel so flattered...so cared for?

She decided she wasn't going to think about that right now. Mark wasn't part of the plan. Instead, Claire opened the door. "Why hello, Miss Tanner, Miss Marchand. What are you doing here?"

Miss Tanner, a thin woman with short gray hair and the constitution of an elephant, as she was fond of saying, put her hands on her hips and scowled. "What do you think you're doing?"

"Excuse me?" Claire asked.

"Flo told us you quit. Tomorrow is Saturday, you know. What do you think you're doing?" she repeated.

"I—"

"How could you?" Miss Tanner interrupted. "People depend on you." She gestured at the comb and scissors. "Unless you've abandoned us for something better." She tried to crane her neck past Claire, probably to see if there was a secret hairdressing shop inside the RV.

"Now, Colleen, calm down," Miss Marchand said. A large woman given to bright-pink floral dresses, she was the more reasonable of the two. "I'm sure Claire has her reasons."

"Dorene can do your hair as well as I can." Claire said.

"No. She can't." Miss Tanner actually pouted. "Besides, she can't stand Sweet Pea and won't let me bring my puppy into the shop like you did." Miss Tanner's "puppy" was a giant Doberman who terrified half the people in town. Claire didn't blame Dorene, a petite hairdresser who could have been a between-meals snack for Sweet Pea.

"It's true, Claire. Dorene tries hard, but she's just not you," Miss Marchand added. "Why *did* you quit?"

Claire took a seat on the step, cradling her scissors and comb in her lap. "I'm moving to California."

Both women gasped. "Whatever for?"

"That's what I've been wondering." Mark squeezed into the space beside her on the step. She was now pressed up against him, inordinately aware of every breath he took, of the warmth of his body, of the dimple on his chin.

"Congratulations to you, Mark," Miss Marchand said. "Those babies of Katie and Matt's are beautiful. I'm so glad I gave that couple a nudge. They're well-suited, if I say so myself."

Claire had heard all the details of Matt and Katie's courtship from the Misses. A very pregnant Katie had stopped in the shop a few weeks ago. She'd glowed and smiled the entire time Claire was working on her hair.

"You've seen them?" Mark asked. To make more room, he had put his left arm behind Claire's back. The temptation to lean against him, to see what his arm would feel like around her waist, to touch him again as she almost had during the haircut, intensified. Awareness, heightened by his closeness, pounded through her veins. She wanted him, and the thought was less of a surprise than she'd expected.

She chanced a glance at Mark. He offered her a soft smile, and despite herself, she returned his smile, before jerking her attention back to The Misses.

"I headed right on up to the hospital, soon as I heard." Miss Marchand said. "It's good those two got married." She cast a pointed look at Claire, then Mark. "Seems a smart move for two young people who are right for each other. Wouldn't you agree?"

Neither Claire nor Mark said a word.

"What about you, Mark? When are you settling down? Your brother Jack's already married and has two kids, Luke has Emily, Katie's got two. I'd say you're next in line."

"Yes, Mark." Claire grinned, delighted to see the tables turned on him. "What about you? When are you going to settle down?" She cast him an innocent smile.

"As soon as I find a woman who knows how to make a killer lemon meringue pie," he answered.

Claire had expected him to say "never." Mark had never been one to come anywhere near a church, never mind a commitment. Once again, she wondered if he'd changed in California. Maybe...

But she dismissed the thought before it could even form itself in her mind.

"Seems to me you don't need to look very far." Miss Marchand muttered. "People always miss what's right under their noses." She cleared her throat, then took Miss Tanner's elbow. "We'd best be going. I wish you luck, Claire."

"I don't." Miss Tanner scowled. "I wish you were back at Flo's. Everything in this town is always changing. I hate it."

Claire bit back a laugh. The Misses waved a goodbye, then walked away, complaining all the while about the dearth of good hairdressers and the tendency of new ones to use not enough hairspray.

"You've got quite the fan club there," Mark said.

"They'll find someone else."

Mark studied her. "I don't know about that. I don't think there's anyone else quite like you."

Claire swallowed hard and got to her feet. Her growing attraction for Mark was due to their constant proximity, nothing more. Getting involved with him would only keep her in the same rut she'd been in since high school. Claire wanted a life. Her own, not the one a man offered her. She knew what his words were implying, she could see the interest in his cobalt eyes, but she wasn't going to go down that path. She headed back into the kitchen and slipped her scissors back into their case.

"You're done," she said when he entered the kitchen.

He ran a hand over his head. "Hey, it feels perfect. Thanks."

"You're welcome." She started to leave.

Mark folded his arms and decided he wasn't going to let her get away that easily. When she'd cut his hair and later, when they'd been together on the step, he knew he hadn't imagined the simmering desire between them. Claire *was* interested in him. Good.

"I should pay you." He grinned. "I can think of many interesting ways to do that. With clothes. Or without."

"No thank you." Claire's annoyance with him was clear.

Once again, his baser nature had escaped like a dog off a chain and made him say the worst possible thing at the worst time. "What do you charge to cut the hair of a complete moron who always says the wrong thing?"

"Nothing."

She'd put up that wall again. Hell, he'd probably helped her lay the bricks. Every time he got close to her, some idiotic statement slipped out of his mouth. "I'm sorry. I'm an idiot. I've asked the Wizard for a brain but it hasn't been delivered yet." He grinned. "Will you accept my apology for saying stupid things and asking you too many personal questions?"

Claire smiled. "Hairdressers don't tell their troubles to their customers. It's usually the other way around."

"If you want, I can hop back into the chair and tell you a thing or two about me. Or, we could switch positions. I could cut your hair while you tell me your problems."

She looked horrified. "I would never let you near my hair with scissors."

"How about if I just pretend?" He stepped forward and took a slip of hair between his fingers. Silk. Blond silk. The urge to haul her close and press his mouth to hers nearly consumed him. He told himself it was enough just to touch her hair.

But it wasn't. He was kidding himself if he thought what he had started to feel for Claire was just friendship. Sometime during the last few days, it had moved way beyond that for him. He wanted her with him, beside him, for everything. Mundane things like washing the dishes and watching the news. Things he'd never considered with any woman before.

"Are you two quite done?" Millie insinuated herself into the small space between Mark and Claire. "I'd like to get a drink of water, if you don't mind freeing up the kitchen for five seconds. And it is lunchtime, you know."

Claire stepped back, out of his reach. "Let me…let me get that mess cleaned up." She reached for the broom and dustpan hanging from a hook by the refrigerator. She hurried over to the chair and began sweeping up what had been on Mark's head five minutes ago.

He put a hand on the broom. "No, you did all the work. The least I can do is clean up." He cocked his head toward the couch. "Go sit down, relax. Watch TV. I'll get this."

Claire crossed to the sofa but perched on the end, looking far from comfortable. She didn't glance his way, instead keeping her gaze on the television.

Just then, James Kent's face appeared on the television screen as part of the noon entertainment report. His grin seemed to take up half the screen. Mark paused in his sweeping. "It's now day six of the Survive and Drive competition at the Mercy Mall," the reporter began. "Only ten contestants remain. Who will win the motor home? The grandma?" A picture of Millie flashed on the screen and she let out a cry of delight. "The newlyweds?" Roger's and Jessica's faces, squished together in a happy harmony shot, were shown. "The beauty?" Claire's image. At least they got that one right. "Or the playboy?"

For that, they put up Mark's face. It wasn't a reputation entirely off base. But it was one he'd been trying to put behind him since California.

Claire shot him a quick glance that he couldn't read. Was it amusement? Irritation? Disappointment?

They flashed photos of Lester, Renee, Danny, Art and Gracie, then finished the report. "Stay tuned as we follow the battle for the chance to win a big-ticket motor home." James Kent's face disappeared from the screen, replaced by an advertisement for Deluxe Motor Homes.

As Mark cleaned up, he thought first about Claire. He remembered now who Leanne Hartford was, though he'd had to go ten years into his past to do it. He hoped like hell Claire didn't see him as the guy who'd broken her friend's heart anymore, but he suspected she did. His past was a hard thing to shed.

Even with his own brother. Luke had always been a nine-to-five kind of guy. Punch in, punch out. Provide for his family. Achieve his goals. Mark had been the complete opposite. But now, after losing everything, he realized that he admired Luke's steadfastness and commitment, and his family. He wondered if it was possible to have the same thing for himself. If he would ever be able to get beyond his past and begin a future.

His thoughts turned to the training program that he and Luke had thought of putting together, before they'd lost the business. For days, he'd been trying to think of a way to market the program as a valuable entity to a business. What would make people pay for a trainer when they could just buy the manuals?

And then it hit him. Claire. The Misses. Relationships. Trust. A lightbulb lit up in his head.

Everyone wanted someone they could depend on, someone who could be a resource for answers, support…training. That was how he could sell this program. That was how he could create the best of both worlds. If he promoted the package as a partnership where businesses could depend on the same trainer, rather than a slew of semiexperts who were gone as soon as the class ended, then he'd have something of value. Let Luke build the software and Mark could be the conduit to helping businesses apply it.

He put the broom and dustpan back on the hook. The others in the room had begun chatting excitedly about their appearances on television, but he barely heard them. The ideas, the wording for the proposal, the possibilities, were churning fast and furious in his mind. He wanted to get back to his laptop before he lost any of it.

But then he noticed Claire, tucked into a corner of the sofa, lost in thought. He'd managed to solve the block with the training program. Maybe…he could solve the block between himself and Claire.

He darted into the back bedroom and returned a moment later, clutching the second tin of cookies. "Here," he said, handing it to Claire.

"What's this?" The smile curved across her face made him wish he had ten more containers of cookies. She pulled the lid off, inhaled the homemade smell. "Your mother always did make the best cookies. Are these peanut butter?"

"Uh-huh."

"Oh God, those are my favorite." She eyed them with undisguised hunger. If she looked at him the way she looked at the cookies, he'd come undone.

"Take as many as you want." *Take them all if you'll keep smiling like that.*

"As many as I want?" Her hand hovered over the stack.

"They're all yours. Consider them a tip for cutting my hair. And a thank-you."

"For the haircut?"

"That and a few other things." For being the inspiration behind his problem's solution. For being on this RV with him. For simply being Claire.

She selected one and took a bite. "Oh…heaven," she said, then took another bite, chewed, swallowed. "But, if I'm eating all the cookies," Claire said between bites, "then what are you going to use as payment to borrow my soap and shampoo again?"

Mark's gaze held hers. A smoldering electricity seemed to carry on the air between them. "I'm sure I'll think of something."

Chapter Six

That afternoon, Mark watched Claire in the kitchen, beating a chocolate mousse into submission. Art and Gracie were napping; Roger and Jessica sat on the couch, arguing about kitchen appliances. Millie knitted another afghan while Lester dozed in the recliner. Renee sat on the floor, playing solitaire. Danny was married to the NFL, of course.

Mark knew he should be thinking about eliminating the competition, but all he saw was Claire. Her hips swayed to the music on the kitchen radio as she worked, a sight more delicious than the dessert she was making. She seemed so at home, so perfect in the kitchen.

For years, he'd avoided anything remotely resembling commitment with women. Then Claire had come back into his life. However, she'd made it clear she didn't want to be tied down to anyone right now. On any other day, Mark would have seen that as an opportunity. But now, he wanted more. He wanted the house, the desserts in the kitchen, the smile at the end of the day.

He wanted Claire.

Claire went on working, clearly unaware of where his thoughts were going. This was her fourth or fifth dessert of the week, concocted from the shopping lists she gave Nancy. All had been equally amazing, especially considering she'd cooked them in a kitchen the size of a breadbox.

He took advantage of her pause in beating and dipped a finger into the bowl to taste the creamy concoction. "This is incredible. Better than the mousse I had in L.A."

"You mentioned you liked mousse, so I made some."

"Thanks."

She shrugged, as if it were no big deal. But the dessert was evidence she'd been thinking of him and that realization pleased him more than he'd thought possible.

He took another taste. "You really are good at this. How come you didn't become a chef?"

She swatted away his hand before he could dip again. "And how would I have gotten to cooking school?"

"Easy. Sign up and go."

"Going to cooking school takes money." She spooned the mousse into ten plastic bowls, then disconnected and washed the beaters. "Which I didn't have much of and Abe wasn't going to part with, not when there was a sale on beer."

With Claire's attention diverted, Mark didn't waste any time. He scooped up another taste from the last little bit in the bowl. "There are scholarships. Financial aid."

"My chance to go to cooking school ended ten years ago. I should have gone. I always wanted to. But I got sidetracked and wound up at beauty school instead." She returned to the counter, grabbed a second bowl out of the cabinet and set it on top of one filled with ice. Then she poured a generous amount of cream into the top bowl.

She dried the clean beaters, reattached them to the hand mixer and began whipping the cream until it foamed. "I wish I had a copper bowl. It works better," she muttered.

As she worked, a look of contentment softened her features. The aroma of the chocolate, coupled with the quiet accent of Claire's perfume, lent an air of home to the scene. She began to hum along with the song on the radio, an old seventies tune. Her ponytail bobbed to the beat as she started to dance a little.

When was the last time a woman other than his mother had cooked for him? Easy—never. Yesterday, he'd complained about the runny pudding sent over by a local restaurant. He'd said he missed the mousse he'd had in L.A. The remark had been made in passing, not meant as a hint for her to make the dessert.

The thought of Claire going the extra mile and cooking a dish she knew he'd like was a nice feeling. Very nice. So domestic, like the scenes he'd witnessed a million times between his parents, and with Luke and Mary.

Watching Claire hum and cook made him realize he craved something more than the chocolate, something far more personal. The pang he'd felt when he'd looked around Luke's room returned to his chest, striking hard and fast.

He wanted Claire. Not just in his bed, but in his life. She'd said so many times that she didn't want him and yet...he sensed the conflict in her. He suspected she'd lumped him into the same pile with the other men who'd broken her heart—men as afraid of commitment as monkeys were of water, Peter Pans who hadn't left Never-Never Land—all because of a few stupid mistakes he'd made when he was young.

With a start, Mark realized he didn't know the adult

Claire all that well. What did she dream of? What did she want? And what had made her afraid of getting involved?

"Claire, are you happy as a hairstylist?" he said.

She shrugged. "It's a job."

"Yeah, a job, but not a career for someone who always dreamed of being a chef."

She shut off the beaters, tested the cream's stiffness, apparently decided it wasn't done, and turned the beaters back on. "What about you? Are you working at what you love?"

"I don't exactly leap out of bed to write software manuals." He laughed. "But there aren't many jobs for what I like to do."

The beaters whirred and whipped. "Which is?"

Mark dipped his finger into the mousse bowl and managed to come up with another glob. "I like talking to people, helping them." Claire glanced at him as he licked the tip of his finger. The beaters skipped against the side of the bowl. Twice. She jerked back to her task. "I hated being a salesman. There was always an ulterior motive for every conversation."

Claire tipped her head and gave him a smile. And as with the beaters, he felt a skip, skip in his chest. "I have to admit, you've been really good at keeping tempers under control on the RV. I never would have thought of that card thing."

He clutched a hand to his chest. "Is that a compliment? From Claire? The same girl who hates my guts?"

The smile disappeared from her face and her whole body seemed to get quiet. "I don't hate you at all." She continued to beat at the cream even though stiff peaks had already formed.

Dare he hope she was starting to feel the same things as he? "Don't take that too far, or you'll ruin it."

She glanced over at him, blinking in confusion. "Wha...What?"

"The whipped cream." He gestured at the bowl, then shrugged. "Hey, my mother constantly watches the food channel. I've learned a thing or two. I may be a guy, but I do know if you overbeat the cream, you'll end up with butter instead."

"Oh. Yeah." A tinge of red appeared on her cheeks. She shut off the mixer, grabbed a spatula off the counter and began scooping the cream onto the bowls of mousse. "I got distracted."

Mark moved closer, until his breath tickled the nape of her neck. A tendril of hair curled across her pale skin, seemingly so innocent, yet so tempting. "Are you saying I distract you?" He kept the teasing tone in his voice but a small part of him wasn't joking. Actually, not a very small part at all.

"Yeah. You do."

"Is that a good thing?"

She nodded, mute. Before he could stop himself or think about what he was doing, Mark bent forward and kissed her neck. Warm, soft skin met his lips, tender and more delicious than anything Claire could ever cook.

Her hand stilled. But she didn't move away. He lingered just a moment, then pulled back. He wanted nothing more than to take her in his arms and kiss her until he forgot his own name, but he knew instinctively that moving too fast would send Claire running for the nearest exit.

"Why...why did you do that?"

"Because I've wanted you for a long time, Claire."

"What, six days and..." She glanced at her watch, "seven hours?"

"Try thirteen years." He leaned against the counter,

giving her a tiny bit more space. "Remember that double date we went on with Jenny and Nate?"

"Yeah. It was a disaster." She laughed, then moved away and placed the mixing bowls into the sink. Her hands trembled and the metal dishes clattered together in a jumble.

"Maybe for you. I had a good time."

"Mark, we barely got along." She turned to get the beaters but he moved to block her. She stopped, her eyes wide, luminous.

"You were so...strong," he said quietly, taking her hand with his. "So confident. So sure of who you were. I envied that in you, and at the same time, it scared the pants off of me. I don't think I've ever known who I am or where I wanted to go."

She let out a shaky laugh. "I'm not sure of anything. You've got me all wrong, Mark."

"Maybe it's you who doesn't see yourself right." He trailed a finger along her throat. She caught her breath, her gaze riveted on his. "You are so much more than you think, Claire. You deserve to be happy."

She yanked her hand back and glanced away. "I'm happy."

"Then why are you so hell-bent on leaving this town and moving half a country away? I know from experience there's nothing in California you can't find here."

"I don't have anything here, Mark. I never did." She swallowed. "The mousse needs to be refrigerated." She grabbed two bowls, thrust them into his hands and fled the kitchen.

"Day Six, later: I've spent most of the afternoon on the phone with Dad," Claire wrote in her journal.

The outlook is no better today. His first round of chemo is only eight days away. I've never wished so badly to be alone. I want to pound a fist through the wall, throw something. But there's no one to get mad at, just some intangible cells taking over my father's body like aliens on an innocent planet.

I could get mad at the tobacco companies, or the cigarettes he smoked, but none of that changes a thing. Every time I call him, I hear a clock ticking faster and faster, telling me to get out there before Dad gets too sick. What if the chemo doesn't work? What if the cancer spreads even further? What if stage two leapfrogs into stage four?

I need to get off this RV. Maybe I should just quit. Leave now, hop on a plane and sort out the rest of the mess called my life later.

"Your turn to cook dinner tonight," Millie chirped as she entered the kitchen. Claire shut her journal with a sigh. "We drew your name out of a hat. You get a helper, though." Millie pulled Mark into the kitchen.

After their conversation over the mousse, she'd done what he'd accused her of doing—she'd escaped. It was far easier to ignore Mark, and all the questions he'd started churning in her mind, than to come up with answers. So she'd immersed herself in her journal and he'd gone back to work, typing madly on his laptop and jotting notes.

But even after several hours hunched over the small computer, he looked energized, ready to take on anything. His hair was mussed and there were shadows under his eyes that said he'd been getting very little sleep lately. Nevertheless, he hummed with energy and strength.

Despite her vow to stay away from him, she felt a sudden urge to lean into him and let him shoulder half her burdens. It was a heavy load—all this worry about her father, her second thoughts about jumping into a new life without much of a safety net, her doubts that any of it would work out. And right now, Mark, clad in a faded denim shirt with the sleeves rolled up, looked capable of handling anything. He'd called her the strong one, but he was wrong. Some days she felt about as strong as a butterfly.

"I'm sure the two of you won't mind working together," Millie said, jolting Claire back to reality. "Make yourselves useful and whip up something good. There's chicken in the bottom drawer of the fridge. Nancy sent it with today's grocery order."

The only person Claire could rely on was herself. She needed to remember that, to focus on that instead of on the electric blue of Mark's eyes and how he looked exactly like the kind of man she'd always pictured in her fantasies. She squared her shoulders and took the apron Millie handed her. She avoided Mark's gaze and concentrated on tying the perfect bow.

"I thought the restaurants provided dinner," he said.

"Only a few restaurants signed up. Tonight, we're on our own." Millie handed him a matching apron, then headed for the couch and a snoring Lester.

The kitchen cubicle was bright enough and cheery, but the view outside the window, Claire decided, was downright depressing. A crowd of people, many of whom she recognized as customers from Flo's, were gathered around the RV. Some were taking pictures, for God's sake, right through the windows.

Claire twirled the blinds shut and turned to face Mark. "We've become a tourist attraction."

He poked a finger through the blinds and peered out.

"Wonder how long it will be before some randy teenager climbs on top and tries to snap a photo through the shower skylight."

"Mark!"

"Hey, I would have done it when I was young."

"You are not the typical guy."

"No?" He stepped closer and for an instant, she thought he was going to kiss her. Against all her common sense, she allowed her gaze to travel over him, taking a moment to admire Mark as a man. He had a strong face, a bit rugged from the time he'd spent under a California sun. His shoulders were broad, capable and clearly well-defined beneath his shirt. His eyes, such a vibrant cobalt color, always seemed to dance with a tease. But right now, there was no teasing in his gaze. Just a liquid burning that seemed to carry through Claire's veins.

The urge to lean into him returned with a fierceness that surprised her. What if...

What if he kissed her? Would that be so bad?

Or so *good?*

This whole day had brought with it a confusing range of emotions. If only she could get out of the RV for a few minutes, maybe she could think. Clear her head. Get the image of Mark out of there. If that was possible. And...if she even wanted to.

He gave her a curious look, then stepped aside and washed his hands in the sink. "Are you saying I'm unique?"

"I'm saying you're weird," she said, stepping into the comfortable shoes of sarcastic Claire, who never gave her feelings away. She waited for him to finish, then washed her own hands, concentrating hard on the task to avoid the teasing in Mark's eyes.

"Pity. I always thought you were above average."

"Spare me the ten-cent pickup lines, Mark. We have work to do." Her focus should be on winning the RV so she could get to California. She shouldn't be thinking about Mark. And about what a kiss from him would be like. Or about what it would be like to be held in his arms, tight against the strength of his chest.

"Ah, yes, dinner. Think we can whip up something that will impress the other eight?"

"If we were smart, we'd give them food poisoning," Claire said. "Get everybody off here fast so I can win this thing."

"Cheer up." Mark took the chicken out of the fridge and put it on the counter. "You can outlast these people. I doubt many of them will stay more than another week."

She slammed her hands on the counter. The others glanced at her. "I don't have that much time," she whispered. "I don't have any time, for God's sake."

"Then why are you still here? Why not go where you need to go and leave this behind?"

"I made a promise. I need the RV to make it happen. I can't break it. I won't break it. It's too important." She got an onion from beneath the sink and began hacking into it. She had no recipe in mind; she just needed to be busy.

"Claire, if you're upset because you'll miss a vacation—"

She wheeled around, the massive butcher knife still in her hand. "Is that what you think I'm worried about?" Out of the corner of her eye, she saw the others watching and lowered her voice. "It's much more than that."

"Tell me."

Trust him. Rely on him, her mind whispered. She turned back to her onions. "It's personal."

"Fine." But his tone made it clear it wasn't fine at all.

Claire dropped the knife onto the cutting board and let out a sigh. ''I didn't mean it that way. I…I don't want to talk about it. Not here, not with…''

Mark began unwrapping the chicken. ''The entire staff of the *National Enquirer* watching us? Not to mention all the people who want to know standing outside?''

''Yes. I'm going to go insane if I have to spend one more day here. It's a fishbowl.''

''I know exactly what you mean.'' He oiled a baking dish and started putting the chicken pieces in. ''It's too bad we couldn't speed up the process of elimination a little.''

''Yeah. Fast forward to the end.'' Claire dumped the onion slices on top of the chicken. She pivoted to the fridge, grabbed a green pepper, rinsed it off, then began slicing. ''Maybe I should quit. Forget the whole contest.''

''You know…'' Mark paused, washing his hands in the sink.

''What?'' She dropped the pepper slices into the dish.

''We worked together on dinner without a word.'' He gestured toward the chicken. ''Imagine what we could create if we actually had a plan.''

''A plan?''

He leaned down and whispered in her ear, his breath warm on her neck. ''For getting the rest of them to leave the RV.''

''Are you proposing what I think you are?''

He kept his voice low, covering the conversation by sprinkling salt and pepper on the dish. ''We work as a team…''

''…and get the other people to give up…''

''…and then duke it out among ourselves when it's down to two.''

Claire chewed on her lip while she chopped. Team up with Mark? Trust him?

He was her only ally on the RV. And he had helped her get on, even though she was number twenty-one. She glanced at the living area—at Art and Gracie, Millie and Lester, Danny, Roger and Jessica and Renee. Essentially strangers. They all had their own reasons for wanting the motor home but none, from what Claire knew, even compared in urgency and need to her own.

With the combined efforts of Mark and herself, maybe it was possible to convince the others to leave quickly. To give herself a chance to keep her promise.

She glanced at Mark, who was dumping a can of cream of mushroom soup on the chicken. They had, using some sort of mental connection, created a decent chicken dish. It wasn't much, but it boded well for them to work together on this.

What did she have to lose? If she was still stuck here in a week with no shot at winning the RV, then she'd use up her savings and fly to California. It wouldn't be the permanent move she'd promised her dad. The few days she'd have with him would probably end up being spent in an antiseptic-scented room while he underwent chemo, but it was better than nothing.

And if she could—maybe—win the RV and drive it out there, pick up her dad and take him on the trip together she'd promised, then it would all be worth it. She'd have her dad; she'd be able to settle down out there afterwards, embark on her new life and have all the time she needed to get to know the man who had fathered her, before losing him—maybe forever.

Suddenly, trusting Mark didn't seem like such a bad idea. He'd said he'd changed, and everything he'd done in the last few days gave weight to those words. He'd become a friend…no, much more than a friend. How much more Claire didn't want to explore, not yet. For now, there was the agreement. She'd puzzle out the rest later.

Claire wiped her hands on a towel, then thrust one out to Mark. "You have a deal."

When they shook, Claire felt something click between them. A link that hadn't been there before.

"Your gift of gab," he winked and she knew he meant no harm, "with my charm. I think we have a winner." He smiled, a long, happy curve that lit up his eyes.

She swallowed and stepped away, breaking the thread between them. "Let's get some potatoes boiling. And after dinner…"

"We execute plan A, whatever that turns out to be."

It was a start. "Okay, tell me what you were thinking," she began, hoping against all hope Mark's idea would work.

And that she hadn't just put her faith in a guy who would let her down, as so many had before.

Plan A, as Mark had called it, consisted of nothing more than annoying and charming the other RV contestants, sort of a Mutt-and-Jeff routine for survival of the fittest. Claire, who could talk a blue streak and never come up for air, would drive them nuts with words. Mark, the smoothest thing to come along since the frappés at the Orchard Restaurant in downtown Mercy, was planning to coax and cajole them right off the motor home.

Or at least, that's what they hoped. As the chicken cooked, they'd talked and planned while they made mashed potatoes and steamed some broccoli. After dinner, they'd volunteered to do the dishes, too, giving them a few more minutes to talk. Running water and the continual drone of the TV kept them from being overheard. By the time the last plate was dried, their plan was sealed. There were few weapons in the Claire/Mark arsenal, but the ones they did have they'd use to their advantage.

Claire finished her soda and tossed the can into the recycle bin. Her thoughts should be on driving people crazy, but they weren't. She kept coming back to Mark, to the odd way he'd looked at her back in the doorway of the RV, and how that look seemed to magnify every time they were together. It was more than lust that she'd read in his eyes, it was almost…longing.

That was crazy. It was just that they were crammed together with a bunch of strangers like sardines in a can. Nothing more.

Claire knew better. She'd seen that hungry look before. It was the kind of interest that convinced a girl to toss away her college education because she believed the guy when he said he loved her, trusted him when he said their love would keep them together, like some corny Sonny-and-Cher routine. Claire took some measure of comfort that a megastar had fallen for the same line of bull she had.

Mark was not settling-down, marriage material. He wasn't even stay-till-morning material. He might have grown up, but she would be kidding herself if she thought for one second that the poster boy for bachelorhood had decided to become a family man. He couldn't have changed that much, not that fast. And Claire had no intentions of knowingly walking into another one of *those* kinds of relationships.

None whatsoever.

No. Not one thought of him. Not the image of his electric-blue eyes. No. Not the feel of his hands at her neck, the warmth of fingers against skin, the tingle when he'd reached *that* place on her nape… *No!* She wouldn't think about it. Wouldn't fall into that trap, the one that began with Mark's lips on hers, nibbling, tasting…

No.

She was most definitely not going to go there. Not even one step down that path.

Millie came into the kitchen and hurried to the fridge. She grabbed a diet soda from the shelf and started bustling back to the sofa. Time to put plan A into action.

"Hey, Millie," Claire said. "How are you doing?"

"Just fine. *The Young and the Rich* is up for a Soap Stars of the Year Award. I so hope Marcie wins."

Claire scrambled for every bit of customer gossip and *TV Guide* trivia she knew. Flo's customers were practically addicted to the show. Claire caught snippets between haircuts, but had never paid close attention. "How long have you been watching?"

"Since November first, nineteen seventy-five." Millie flushed with pride. "I've been with Jace and Marcie since the very first day."

Once, curious about the draw of the number-one-rated soap, Claire had read an article on the show. A few details came back. "You must have seen Marcie's baby born."

The commercial ended. The swirling award announcing the show appeared. "Yes, I did. Cute little booger."

"I heard he was played by twins."

"Yes, he was. Oh! Look, it's back on! Time to see if Marcie finally gets her award." Millie's words were final. The conversation was over. Millie walked back to the couch.

Later, Claire tried the talk-their-ears-off-and-drive-them-off-the-house-on-wheels tactic with Art and Gracie. She seated herself beside them as they played Scrabble and was grudgingly invited into the game. Throughout their battles over three-point squares and double word scores, Claire talked. She expounded on the new shop in the mall, the price of coffee beans, even the reasons why she thought the Scrabble tiles were designed as little squares. She ignored the irritated looks Art and Gracie sent her way, pretended she didn't hear Millie shush her when Marcie made her thank-you speech. She just kept on talking.

Finally, Art and Gracie got fed up, packed up their game and headed for the back bedroom for a bit of privacy. There, they encountered Mark, who was working on his laptop, papers strategically spread across the entire bed. Claire lingered in the kitchen, ostensibly fixing a plate of nachos, but really eavesdropping on their conversation.

"I can't stand this tub anymore, Gracie girl," Art said with an irritated sigh. Gracie murmured agreement.

"It is tough, isn't it?" Mark's voice was all sympathy. "Makes me wonder if it's worth it to stay here and put up with all of…this." Claire peeked around the corner and saw him make a sweeping gesture of the vehicle.

"Exactly what I was thinking," Art replied. "Gracie, maybe we should think about just buying one of these. We don't need one this big, not for the two of us."

"But, Art…"

"Gracie, we could take that CD out of the bank and have an RV of our own in a couple days."

Gracie looked ready to protest, but Mark came to the rescue. "And be on your way to Florida before the cold weather settles in. The *Farmer's Almanac* says this winter is supposed to be one of the worst on record. Lots of snow. Temperatures below freezing. Those biting winds that get under your coat." Mark shook his head and wrapped his arms around himself, as if he were cold.

Gracie actually shivered. "Maybe that's a good idea," she told Art. "Do you think we could get one with a satellite dish, though? I'd sure hate to miss my shows while we're driving."

"Anything you want, sweetheart." Art, a bear of a man, put his arm around petite Gracie's shoulders. They'd been married more than forty years, Art had said earlier. Every one of those years showed in the gentle affection he gave her, in the way he looked at his wife, clearly seeing her with young eyes despite their advanced age.

For some people, love worked out, Claire thought. Not for her, but it was nice to know some people had happy endings.

Art and Gracie entered the kitchen. Claire got busy sprinkling cheese on the nachos. "Well, missy, seems we're not so patient in our old age. We've decided to buy our own instead of waiting for this one to empty out."

Claire shook Art's hand, accepted a hug from Gracie, and wished them well. She saw a gleam of victory in Millie's eyes when she bid them goodbye. She punched Lester to wake him up and get him to say his piece, too. Danny gave a grunt, then went back to the sports section in the newspaper. Roger and Jessica came up for air just long enough to say "hey man" to Art, then went back to the only honeymoon they could get in front of a crowd. Renee was busy with a crossword puzzle and barely gave them a passing glance.

That kind of send-off did not sit well with Millie. At her very persistent insistence—to the point of hauling some people out of their seats—the remaining eight formed a semicircle and said goodbye in unison. As Art and Gracie departed the RV, Ten-Spot News and Nancy Lewis boarded. The lights for the camera were already blazing; James Kent had his mike at the ready.

.

The look on Nancy's face bordered on fury. She marched up to the group, hands on hips. "One of you is lying to us. You'll be packing your bags and leaving. Immediately."

Chapter Seven

Mark's breath got stuck somewhere between his lungs and his windpipe. He stood stone still, waiting for James to shove a microphone in his face, to let the bright lights and accusations come. The thought of that burden being lifted off his shoulders was almost welcome. To be stripped of the accolades he'd never deserved, revealed as an ordinary man who hadn't achieved much in his nearly thirty years on the planet, would be a relief.

James stalked up to him, then right past him. Past Claire. Past Millie and Lester, past Danny, who looked bored. Past Roger and Jessica, who were holding hands and looking a bit nervous. He came to a halt in front of Renee.

"Would you like to tell us anything?" Nancy asked. She held up a sheaf of papers. "Like why you lied on this application?"

"I...I...I didn't lie." Renee's face flushed.

"Do you even *have* a living grandparent?"

Renee ducked her head. "No. But—"

"Did you know there's a warrant out for your arrest from the Lawford Police Department?" James, clearly eager to break his story—and his subject—consulted his ubiquitous notebook. "For driving with a suspended license, driving an uninsured car, leaving the scene of an accident after you crashed your car. Not to mention several hundred dollars' worth of unpaid parking and speeding tickets." He thrust the microphone under Renee's chin.

"We certainly aren't going to award this fine motor home to someone who routinely broke the laws of the road!" Nancy cut in.

As if she'd just realized she'd be all over the local news, Renee shoved the camera away, bonking the cameraman on the head. She darted into the back, grabbed her suitcase and ran out the door. She didn't make it far. Two Lawford police officers greeted her outside the RV and relieved her of her case before leading her away.

James Kent grinned like a lottery winner. He tipped his head toward the cameraman. "Make that the lead for five o'clock. The public will eat it up."

"Don't paint the mall as the responsible party," Nancy said. "We didn't do criminal background checks, for God's sake. We just read over the applications."

"Oh no, I'd *never* exploit the mall for a story."

Mark could practically see the lie whistle by James's teeth. The man was a rat—a rat with ambition. A rat like that could be useful though, Mark thought.

James raised the mike again, signaled to the cameraman, and slipped into his Walter Cronkite voice. "Here we are, at the end of grueling day six in the Survive and Drive contest at the Mercy Mall. After a hasty exit by Renee Angelo, we're down to seven. Seven people locked together in a battle for an eighty-five-thousand-dollar motor home. What's your strategy?'' Before she could protest, James thrust the microphone at Millie.

"I don't really have one. I've just enjoyed being here and meeting all these fine people.''

Mark barely contained his snort of laughter.

James moved on to Lester, who snuck in a howdy to the grandkids. James was at Mark's side in a millisecond. "Hello again, Mr. Dole. Tell me, what's your strategy for winning?''

Like he would tell this weasel. "Longevity. I hear sticking it out is what works.''

James chewed on his lip, clearly mulling a change in tack. "With such beautiful women on board, aren't you tempted to—''

"This is a contest, not an HBO special.''

James frowned, tried again. "I hear you and Claire Richards go back a long ways. Childhood buddies and all that.''

"We know each other,'' was all he conceded.

"I'm sure she knows about your heroic ice rescue. Maybe I should ask her.'' James tipped the mike in Claire's direction.

"Leave her out of this.''

"Why? I'm sure she's got some stories to tell about you.'' He grinned. "You know, I was reading the newspaper accounts of that rescue, and something,'' he paused, tapping a finger against his chin, "something bothers me about it.''

"What happened twenty years ago has nothing to do with this RV competition.''

"Oh, but I think it does. People might not be so inclined to give up their seat to a hero if they realize he isn't actually made of gold.''

Mark mentally counted to ten so he wouldn't slug

James. He'd gotten as far as three when Claire appeared at his side.

"You've known Mark all your life." James thrust the microphone at her. "Does that make it harder to compete?"

"No. But it does give me the advantage of already knowing what makes him tick." Claire offered James a sweet but firm smile. "Of course, Mark has the same advantage over me." She gestured toward Roger and Jessica before the reporter could ask another question. "You know, those two newlyweds don't look too happy. You should ask them how their 'honeymoon' is going."

With one last look at Mark, James crossed to Roger and Jessica, who were now arguing under their breath.

"Thanks," Mark said. "I owe you one."

"No, you don't." She gave him the same smile she'd given the reporter a second ago. "It's all part of plan A." Claire walked away.

Before Mark could follow, Nancy sidled up beside him. She assumed a flirty pose and gave him a very friendly hello. "How's the competition going for you?"

"Fine, just fine." He craned his neck and saw Claire chatting it up with Danny. She never even looked his way.

"I know this is awfully forward of me to ask, but…" Nancy laid a hand on his arm. "How about you and I go out to dinner after all this is over?"

Mark's gaze sought out Claire again. He'd offered her the same thing more than once, and had been shot down like a deer on opening day of hunting season. Every time he tried to get close, Claire rebuffed him. She clearly had no interest in him as anything other than a chess piece helping her take over the board. For some reason, the thought of her wanting him only to execute plan A bothered him more than he thought possible, even though it had been his idea.

He returned his gaze to Nancy. She watched him with the same adoration as all the women he'd known before. All but one.

Knowing he shouldn't do it, knowing he was falling back into the familiar patterns that had landed him here in the first place, Mark offered Nancy his best smile. He might as well face facts—he hadn't changed anymore than the fickle Indiana weather. "Sure. Dinner would be great."

The hound had returned. But he felt more like a dog.

Claire sent up a prayer of gratitude when James Kent finally exited the RV. Although he hadn't interrogated her as he had Mark, his presence was enough to set her teeth on edge. He'd followed everyone around for a couple of hours, sticking the camera into every nook and cranny, trying to get a "taste of life on the RV," he said. Claire didn't know who was worse—the annoying reporter or the too-cheery mall director.

Nancy Lewis. She was gone now, too, offering a final smile at Mark before she shut the door. Claire had overheard their conversation and wanted to gag. Mark hadn't changed a bit. Why had she thought he was different now? Why had she started to believe him when he'd told her he'd grown up?

And why was she so damned disappointed to realize she'd been right?

She knew why. Because some people—namely herself—didn't outgrow their own stupidity. It was the same trap she'd been caught in at eighteen when she'd let Travis talk her into staying in Mercy instead of going to college. Blue eyes and sexy voices were trouble.

Then why did she keep forgetting that every time Mark was near? She hugged her arms to her chest and wished her heart would stop feeling like a shattered piece of glass.

"It's getting late. We should draw again for the beds," Mark announced, holding the deck of cards aloft. "With only seven of us, no one has to sleep on the floor."

He walked around the room, letting each person pick a card. Millie got an ace, Lester, a king. With a smile of triumph, they opted for the bed in back. Lester let out a long and loud yawn, then shuffled off to bed, with Millie chattering alongside him.

Roger and Jessica had the next highest cards and immediately claimed the bed over the cab. Claire saw the almost drooling anticipation in their eyes and figured the entire motor home was in for a long night. The newlyweds giggled and dashed up the ladder. Claire doubted there'd be more than a two-second delay before they were expressing their "undying love" with gusto. She imagined them hanging the RV version of a Do Not Disturb sign: Don't Come A-Knockin' When the Truck's A-Rockin'.

Danny dropped his queen into Mark's hand. "I'm taking the chair up front. It's got the good TV," he said. He crossed to it, propped his feet on the dash and immediately took up residence with the television and the NFL again.

The lights in the mall clicked off, leaving the RV bathed in its own amber lights. Mark and Claire were more or less alone, in the living room and facing each other. "I got a jack," she said, holding up her jack of clubs.

"Me, too." He showed her a jack of hearts.

"Not quite how I'd describe you," she said, nodding at his card. He smiled and for a second, the room seemed closer, tighter. Claire cleared her throat and handed her

card to Mark. "Well, I guess I'll take the chair again."
But she didn't move.

"No, I'll take it. You take the sofa bed." But he didn't
move, either.

Claire let out a shaky laugh. "Guess neither one of us
wants the concrete chair." She lowered her voice.
"There's always the Dallas Cowboys." She gestured toward Danny.

"I don't think so." Mark tap-tap-tapped the cards into
a pile. If Claire didn't know better, she'd say he was stall-
ing. She felt her breath catch in her throat.

"Listen," he said finally, "we're both adults. We can
share the sofa bed and not go wild like a bunch of teenagers. That way, we both get a good night's sleep."

She glanced at the sofa and knew it would be a better
choice than the chair. Her neck had resumed its aching,
as if to remind her it wanted a flat surface and a good
pillow. "We shouldn't. It wouldn't be—"

"Proper?" Mark arched an eyebrow. "Since when did
Claire Richards ever worry about propriety?"

"Never." She let out a soft laugh. The bed was tempting. Broad enough for two. Comfortable enough to give
her the sleep she so desperately craved.

But then she remembered Mark and Nancy, making
plans for a dinner date. Above her, she could hear the
slurpy sounds of Roger and Jessica starting on their honeymoon. Moans, declarations of love. Her mind replaced
the image of the newlyweds with Mark's and Nancy's
faces. A surge of something—she refused to call it jeal-
ousy—reared inside her. "The chair is fine," she said.
"In fact, I prefer it."

Mark grinned at her. "You're stubborn."

"No, I'm just not falling for the Mark Dole line of
seduction. Nancy might have flipped for your smile, but

I'm not that easy a sell.'' She snorted. "A platonic night in the same bed, indeed.''

"Are you…'' he eyed her quizzically in the half light of the RV, "jealous?''

"Are you nuts?'' She shook her head for emphasis. "I'm going to go get ready for bed—'' she stopped herself, realizing how intimate those words sounded, and started again. "I'm going to gargle a little, spit out some toothpaste and change into a ratty T-shirt. Save me one of those pillows, if you don't mind.'' She stalked off before he could argue with her.

When she returned a few minutes later, Mark had curled his six-foot frame into the recliner, his eyes shut, a blanket drawn up to his chin. He looked about as comfortable as an armadillo in a bowling alley. The sofa bed was out and ready for her. Even the corner of the blankets had been pulled back.

Something softened in Claire's heart. She bit her lip, trying to push back the sudden wave of emotion. "You didn't have to do that just because I'm a woman,'' she said. He continued feigning sleep. "I could have slept in the chair again and been just fine.''

Without opening his eyes, he said, "Sometimes, I'm a nicer guy than you think I am. Now go to sleep and leave me alone.'' But there was no irritation in his voice, just a funny tone that sounded an awful lot like…hurt.

No, not possible. Claire climbed into the bed and turned out the light beside her. But sleep refused to come—no matter how comfortable the mattress.

Claire had been right. The chair was made of concrete. Maybe steel. It had to be the most uncomfortable place Mark had ever slept. Well, next to the floor he'd slept on the first and third nights. He could be over there, in bed, with Claire. She had rolled over in her sleep and her T-shirt had ridden up to her hips, exposing one leg. One creamy, silk-smooth leg.

Now he *really* couldn't sleep. Maybe he should cover her. She could be cold, after all. Yeah, that was it. *Claire* was cold. It wasn't that he had solar heat running through his veins at the sight of her leg, oh no, that wasn't it at all.

He got silently to his feet and crossed to the couch. For a second, he just watched her. In sleep, she looked almost…angelic. Normally, that wasn't how he'd describe Claire, but right now, she appeared as vulnerable as a child, curled on her side with a pillow tucked beneath her head. So sweet, so perfect.

Lord, she was a beautiful woman. All legs and long, golden hair. Why she'd ever thought being tall was a curse, he didn't know. He liked a woman who could stand toe-to-toe with him, mentally and physically. He realized now, looking down at the woman who had made his life an interesting living hell, that he'd grown tired of women like Nancy, who saw his looks and nothing else.

They didn't know him, really know him, the way Claire did. There'd never been a history with the other women. All they'd wanted was today. A good time, a man without strings. Easy conquests, he thought. No challenge involved. No risk of failure—no risks at all. Those words summed up how Mark had lived his life—until just recently.

So why the hell had he agreed to dinner with Nancy? Was he just hell-bent on ruining his own life? Not to mention any possible shot with Claire? Or was he afraid of taking that step forward, one that might lead to something substantive? As much as he said he wanted the life Luke had had with Mary, and what Katie had with Matt

and the twins, moving toward it was damned near terri-
fying. It meant being responsible. Dependable. Could he
be that man? He hadn't been that man on the ice twenty
years ago. He hadn't been that man when Luke needed
him.

That last mistake had been the wake-up call he'd
needed, though. Since then, he'd had a goal and had been
working toward it—to make enough money to start their
company again, between the sale of the RV and his pay
for writing those manuals. That felt good. Having a mission, a destination, was a great feeling. It gave a man
direction. The one thing he'd been searching for all his
life—but never known he needed. Until now.

Mark shook himself, dismissing those thoughts, along
with the illicit ones about how beautiful and tempting
Claire looked. She'd said he couldn't keep it platonic between them. Well, he'd show her. He reached for the blanket pooled at the bottom of the bed and started to cover
her.

As he did, she stirred and rolled over. "What are you
doing?" Her voice was husky with sleep, veering his
thoughts into bedroom territory again. How could one
question sound so damned sexy?

So much for keeping his thoughts platonic. "You,
ah…you looked cold." He held up the blanket in a lame
explanation.

"Oh." She sat up on her elbows. "Thanks."

"No problem." He clutched the blanket a minute
longer, then realized how stupid he looked standing there
with one of Millie's afghans in his hands. He leaned forward and draped the multicolored cover over her legs.
"There."

A smile curved across her face. "Thanks."

"Don't mention it." He turned to go back to the chair but stopped when she spoke again.

"I wondered about that," she said softly.

He pivoted back. "About what?"

She started, and it was clear she hadn't meant to speak the words aloud. "About whether you were ah...a..."

"What?"

She lowered her gaze. "Whether you were a boxers or briefs guy."

"Oh." He grinned, then pointedly looked down at the plaid fabric shorts. He had been hot crammed into the chair and had removed his sweats a while ago, figuring he could slip back into them before he got up in the morning. "Get your answer?"

She raised her head again, emerald eyes sweeping over the same area. "Uh-huh."

Even with just the soft glow of a nightlight behind her, Mark could swear he saw tinges of red in Claire's face. Imagine that. Claire was rarely embarrassed by anything, least of all the sight of a near-naked man. She'd been the scorekeeper for the football team in high school and had had few qualms about popping into the locker room to clear up a stat. Always, she'd averted her eyes, but the teenage boys on the team, intent on preserving their image of being strapping men, had cringed in embarrassment. Then she'd crack a joke and set them all at ease.

"I haven't seen you in your underwear for years," she said, then let out a laugh as if she'd realized how that sounded. "Since you were on the football team, I mean."

"I'm a bit bigger now." He let the double meaning remain.

"Yeah." Her face darkened. "You are."

"Well, good night then." He went back to the chair.

"Mark?"

Her voice sounded so sweet, like a piece of candy waiting for him across the room. "Yeah?"

"You can't be comfortable in that chair. If you promise to be a good boy," and the teasing Claire came back into her words, "then you can sleep here. With me."

Concrete chair or share a bed with Claire? Mark didn't hesitate. In two seconds, he was flat on his back and easing into comfort. "Claire, you are a goddess."

She leaned over him, pointing a finger at his face. In the dark, her emerald eyes were wide and luminous, twin dark pools that seemed to draw him in. "No hands. No mouth. Not even a foot brushing up against my leg. Okay?"

"Yes, ma'am. I'll be on my best behavior." He saluted her and stiffened himself into a straight line as proof. "That goes for both of us, you know."

"You think I can't keep my hands to myself?"

"I think you're crazy about me and afraid to admit it."

She rolled back, facing away from him. "Careful, Mark, your ego is showing." But there wasn't any malice in her tone.

"You're keeping me awake," he whispered. "Now go to sleep. And try not to dream about me."

She laughed and snuggled closer to the other edge. She could have been five hundred feet away and he couldn't have been more aware of her if he tried. The picture of her—T-shirt raised, leg flung across the bed—ran through his mind like a movie stuck replaying the same scene.

Mark clung to his side of the bed, gripping it to prevent himself from rolling over and drawing Claire to him. He pictured that creamy leg draping over his, the soft crush of her against his chest, that kiss-me mouth turning the tables and leaving a trail of tender nibbles along his neck, down his chest…

The sound of moaning came from above the cab. Mark burrowed his head into the pillow. The sounds got louder, with desperate pleas for "More, Jessica" and intermittent cries of "Oh, Roger." Lord, these people must have learned Lovemaking 101 from Al's Video Shop.

And then, came the rhythmic squeak-squeak-squeak of the bed above. Grunts, groans, sounds of pleasure. Mark shut his eyes, but that only made it worse. With his eyes closed, all he saw was the image of Claire, wanting, needing more…

Mark dug his fingers into the side of the bed, gripping the metal frame. Every inch of him ached, not in pain, but in a desperate longing for the woman less than three feet away.

"Roger!" Jessica's cry made no secret of the magic her new husband had just wrought.

Mark gritted his teeth and tried to picture *anything* but what was going on in the cab above them and what he'd like to be doing with Claire. Why had he been such an idiot? Going back to those stupid lines when he'd asked her out, like some kind of crutch. No wonder she'd said no. And then, asking Nancy out…how dumb was that? In the morning, he'd tell Nancy dinner was off. When this competition was over, he would convince Claire that he wasn't the same guy she'd grown up with.

Though whether she'd still talk to him after he won the RV, he wasn't sure. But oh, how he wanted her to. How he wanted to redeem himself—in his own eyes, and in hers.

The squeak-squeak-squeak started in earnest again. Roger was young. This could go on for hours.

Mark clutched the pillow to his head but remained attuned to Claire, to every breath, every movement. Five minutes ago, the bed had seemed pretty damned comfortable. Now it was a torture chamber.

Chapter Eight

Claire lay in the dark and waited for morning. With Mark only a few feet away, her brain refused to turn off. Every sound compounded her insomnia, from the muffled hock-hock of Lester's snores to the mumbles of Danny talking in his sleep. All seemed amplified and annoying.

Roger and Jessica had finally hit the pause button on their honeymoon. As far as Claire could tell, they'd passed out from exhaustion. Thank God.

"Mark? Are you asleep?" she whispered, then rolled over to check for herself.

He was practically teetering on the brink of the bed, his entire body one straight, stiff line parallel to the edge. "No."

She let out a sigh. "I can't sleep."

"Try counting sheep."

"Did that."

"Try telling yourself a bedtime story."

"I don't know any."

He flipped to his back. "Come on, everyone knows a

bedtime story. Try anything—''Rapunzel,'' ''The Ugly Duckling.'' What did your mother tell you when you were a kid?''

Claire picked at an errant thread on the afghan. ''She didn't. When I was little, she was always sick. As soon as I was old enough, I put myself to bed.''

''And Abe wasn't exactly the storytelling type.''

''Oh, he told stories. The type you hear in a brothel.''

Mark laughed. ''Not much of a father figure, huh?''

She snorted. ''Not even close.'' She folded her pillow to make it higher then lay down again, facing Mark. In the dark, the barriers of daytime dropped away. The world seemed to consist of just her and Mark, bringing a closeness, an edge to their friendship that wasn't there under the harsh lights of day. She forgot about Nancy, forgot about her resolve to stay away from him. Right now, she was cold, awake and lonely. And Mark was here, with her, listening. ''Can I ask you something?''

''Shoot.''

''Why are you here? I mean, you don't seem the Disneyland type and you don't have kids, so why do you need this RV?''

He didn't say anything for so long, she wondered if he'd gone back to sleep. The ticking of the kitchen clock noted the passing seconds of silence, heavy and thick. ''Because I screwed up royally and I need to fix my mistake.''

''Come on. Mark Dole doesn't screw up. He's the boy who can do no wrong.''

He laced his hands behind his head. ''You don't know me that well, Claire.''

''Sure I do. You've won at everything you've ever attempted. Homecoming king, state track, scholarships.

Face it, ever since you rescued that boy, you've been like King Midas.''

Mark ran a hand over his face and let out a sigh that seemed to weigh a thousand pounds. ''I didn't...'' He swallowed, started again. ''I didn't rescue Kenny.''

''What do you mean? It was all over the papers. An eleven-year-old fell in when he was skating on a private pond. You were there and pulled him out even though you were a year younger and a lot smaller.''

''It didn't work that way.'' Mark closed his eyes and when he did, he was transported back two decades. A cold day, a fresh patch of ice. His favorite hockey stick, the one his dad had bought him for Christmas, slung over his back as he tromped into the woods to a secluded patch of ice. Finding another boy there—a bully from school. ''I ran into Kenny Higgins when I got out to the pond behind the Emery Farm. Few people knew about that pond because it was so far back from the road. I'd found it one summer when I was looking for a frog to put in my sister's bed.''

''You put a frog in your sister's bed?''

Mark chuckled. ''That's a brother's mission in life—to torture squeamish sisters.''

''It must have been nice.'' Claire let out a long breath.

''Nice? To have a frog in your sheets?''

''No. To have a brother.'' She gave him a bittersweet smile. ''I'm the only one of my kind, you know.''

He heard the attempt at levity in her voice, the joke edged with pain. He let it pass, knowing intuitively Claire's close-to-orphan life was a sore spot. ''Katie never thought it was so great, but I guess she's changed her mind. After all, she did marry a guy and just had a son and a daughter.''

''I'm happy for her.'' She paused. ''I'm sorry. I got

you off track, didn't I?'' In the dark, her eyes seemed bigger, brighter. Prettier. ''Go back to the story about the ice.''

''I'd rather talk about putting amphibians in my sister's bed.'' But even as he said it, Mark knew if he didn't start letting the truth come out, he'd never move past that day. Maybe if his image was finally tarnished, people would stop expecting him to be anything more than a human who screwed up more than he liked to admit. That thought was almost a welcome one, as if he could see the place where he could lay his burden.

''When I got to the ice and saw Kenny there, I was mad,'' Mark began. In the dark, it became easier to confess to Claire. The night offered a veil of comfort, of acceptance of his flaws. ''Kenny and I had never gotten along. He was the last person I wanted to see.'' He flattened against the mattress, propping his head with his hands. ''He grabbed my new hockey stick and took off with it before I could get my skates on. I ran after him and we got into a fight. I shoved him pretty hard and grabbed my stick back as he...''

When he didn't finish, Claire filled in the blank. ''He fell through the ice.''

''Yeah.'' Mark sighed. ''It was fresh ice and the middle wasn't all the way hard yet. I saw Kenny in there, flailing around, being pulled down by his winter clothes and I wanted to do anything to take that shove back.''

''So you pulled him out?''

He shook his head. ''I started to, but Kenny cursed me up and down for pushing him. He told me he could get out himself. The ice started to crack under me when he grabbed at the edge and I panicked, so I...'' Mark's sentence trailed off. These were the harder words to say, the biggest mistake to admit.

Tick. Tock. Tick. Tock. The clock, the very air seemed to be waiting for him to finish.

"So I ran away."

"You left?" Claire's voice was pitched with surprise.

He turned and looked at her. "I told you, I'm not this demigod everyone makes me out to be. I'm a guy who happened to get lucky a few times in his life." Whether that luck had been deserved or not, he amended mentally.

"But how did Kenny get out of the water?"

"I ran away, but I didn't get far, just to the bank of the pond. My conscience wouldn't let me. Deep down inside, I knew help was too far away. I could hear the ice cracking. It sounded like popcorn popping. Crack. Crack. Crack. I looked back and I saw Kenny go down. He didn't come back up right away. I ran to him, out of instinct, I guess. He bobbed back up, thank God, and started to cry. Really cry. I knew he wasn't going to make if I didn't help. I lay down on the pond, handed him one end of my stick. It took some doing, but I pulled him out. I swear I never ran so fast in my life as I did for that edge after I got Kenny out. The ice just shattered behind us."

"But why wasn't any of that in the story we all heard?"

"Kenny made a deal with me. He was the older one, you know, and he had a reputation for being tough. The last thing he wanted people to know was he'd cried like a baby when he fell in the water. I wasn't too keen on people knowing I'd walked away, so we made up our own version."

"And both of you have stuck to it ever since?"

Mark nodded. "To be honest, I wish we'd never lied."

"Why?"

He sighed. "All my life, people have pointed to me as a hero. I'd go into Harper's Ice Cream Parlor and Mr. Harper would make me a sundae before I even sat down.

In school, teachers would let me get away with things other kids couldn't. Mercy's a small town. People never forget what you do in a small town, good or bad." He shook his head. "But I never was a hero. I never wanted to be." What was it James Kent had called him? Made of gold. Claire had called him King Midas. "Being made of gold makes for a damned heavy load to carry."

"But you never corrected people, either. You never stepped up and told them not to do any of those things."

There it was again—Claire's pinpoint accuracy for the truth. She was right. He'd let the story grow into monumental proportions, allowed the accolades to become a daily part of his life. He'd always been afraid, just as he was today, that he couldn't really make it on his own. That he hadn't quite found his niche in life, not as easily as Luke had.

"No, I didn't correct them." He ran a hand through his hair and faced a few things about himself. "I'm not going to lie to you, Claire. When you're a teenager, that kind of attention is just what your ego ordered. By the time I was in high school, that story had grown so much, I could have driven the principal's car through the front door and people would have said I was trying to rescue a kitten. Because of that, I never had to try hard. I got A's because some teacher thought I was college material. My life was easy. I wasn't going to protest if people let me skate by." Luke had worked hard for everything he'd ever attained. With the wisdom of a few years behind him, Mark realized he envied that about his brother.

"But still, you did save Kenny."

"Reluctantly, Claire. That doesn't make me much of a savior."

"You were a kid. You're not expected to be an ideal citizen at ten."

"Either way, I shouldn't have walked away. They say a man's character shows true in times of crisis and I, well…" His voice dropped several notches. "I know where mine lies."

Claire put a hand on his arm. Warmth infused him, racing through his veins. "I think you expect more of yourself than anyone else ever has."

He thought of how he had disappointed Luke. "I've never expected enough." Mark drew the blanket to his chest, displacing Claire's touch. "Maybe we should get some sleep."

"You never answered my question."

He closed his eyes. "What's that?"

"Why do you want to win the RV?"

He rolled over. "Because last year, I let someone else down and this is my chance to make it up."

"What are you talking about?"

"I thought you wanted a bedtime story," he said, flipping back to face her. "This one doesn't end happily. Not yet."

"That's okay." She lay back on her pillow and watched him in the dark. Waiting patiently. Claire wouldn't push him or nag him into talking. If he said he didn't want to talk about it, she'd let it go at that. It was just the kind of woman she was. He respected that—respected her.

Telling her about Kenny had lightened his soul a tiny bit. Maybe telling her about his mistake with Luke would do the same.

He took a deep breath before beginning. "Five years ago, Luke and I went out to California to start our own business. It was mainly Luke's idea, and at that point, I was just along for the ride." He shrugged. "Luke was pretty much the brains behind everything. All I did was help sell his ideas.''

"I don't know about that," Claire said quietly. "You're a smart guy yourself."

"Not smart enough. At least not when it counted." He punched his pillow back into shape, then lay down again. "We did really well for four-and-a-half years. Luke was working insane hours, which drove Mary crazy. They fought about it all the time, but you know my brother— that's how he is. When he gets into something, he's so focused the rest of the world disappears. He buried himself in the business and did a lot of the administrative stuff on top of the software design."

"So what did you do?"

"What I did best. Sell. Luke's not a real social person—"

"The complete opposite of you," Claire inserted.

"Yeah. You'd never know we were twins by our personalities." Mark grinned. "Anyway, I did all the selling, and, like I said, it worked well for four-and-a-half years. Then the dot-com world started to implode and business began to get a little shaky. We had just landed a big contract, though, so we thought we were safe. We even brought on a couple of new employees to help with the software writing. Luke needed to order faster and better computers, so we had this huge equipment lease, plus the extra programmers to pay." Mark noticed Claire had inched closer to him as he talked. A warm feeling settled over his heart. "Anyway, the new contract meant Luke was spending even more hours at work, which didn't set well with Mary, understandably. They started fighting like crazy. Then the customer began hemming and hawing about a completion date. When they fell behind on payment, we suspected something might be up, but kept on working because we thought it was temporary.''

''But it wasn't, was it?''

Mark shook his head. ''Then Mary was killed by a drunk driver. Luke was devastated. He handed over all the books and everything he was doing for the company and asked me to take care of it. There was the funeral and Emily and…I think he felt incredibly guilty. He just retreated into a shell and barely came into the office.''

''So you had to do all the administrative and management things on top of selling?''

''Yeah. I figured I could do it. I had been to college for business, but—'' Mark let out a breath. ''In the end, the business went down the tubes. The big contract we'd been counting on fell through. The customer filed bankruptcy. We were left holding the bills with no way to pay them. If I'd sold more or tried something else, maybe this wouldn't have happened.''

''Mark, a lot of software companies went out of business that year. Surely you can't think—''

''If I'd been more on top of things, I wouldn't have let this happen. I could have…I could have done something. *Anything.* Luke was counting on me. Guess he picked the wrong guy, huh?'' Mark let out a bitter laugh.

Claire slid across the bed and laid her head beside his. She pressed a hand to his cheek and stared into his eyes. ''You didn't let the company down, Mark. It wasn't your fault.''

He jerked away and sat on the edge of bed. ''It was just like with Kenny, only this time there was no rescue at the end.'' He dropped his head. ''We lost it all. The bank took back the computer equipment, the office building rescinded our lease. We had to pay the programmers for their contract, and that took every dime we had. Then of course, we couldn't afford to stay in California and nobody was hiring idiot entrepreneurs, so we came back home.''

Claire wrapped her arms around his chest. Mark blinked several times to get rid of the sting in his eyes. She laid her head on his shoulder and then softly kissed his neck.

A feeling of security, of acceptance, invaded his heart. Claire. How had he ever gotten so lucky to meet her? With her against him, he felt the weight of his guilt lift. She hadn't recoiled when he'd told her about Kenny, hadn't shut him out when he'd talked about losing the company. Instead, she'd taken him into her arms and accepted him, warts and all.

Wasn't this exactly what he'd been seeking? How could he have missed this, missed her, all these years? Right here, right in Mercy, was the woman he'd always wanted.

He sat there, drawing from the strength of her embrace. There was acceptance there. True friendship. Something that almost bordered on…love.

''You did the best you could,'' she said. ''You can't keep blaming yourself.''

''Yes, I can.'' Mark turned and faced her. That blame had been the fuel for pursuing his goal. ''I've been saving the money I make from writing manuals, but it isn't enough. If I can win the RV, I can sell it and have enough cash to get the business started again. I figure I'll have five months of operating capital left over, which should be enough to get us back on our feet.'' He lay back down and Claire did the same. He draped the blanket over both of them and she snuggled closer.

How he wanted to take her in his arms, to draw Claire to him. But he didn't because he wasn't sure how she felt yet. She might push him away and all these new feelings between them would be lost.

"And what if you don't win the RV?"

"I'll cross that bridge when I get to it," Mark said quietly. "In the meantime, I'm throwing a few more boats in the water, just in case."

A beach. Warm, velvety sand beneath her skin. A soft, gentle breeze tickling her hair. Claire let out a contented sigh in her dream. It was a perfect setting. Except the warm sand was rising and falling with a continual steadiness.

When she moved, she realized she wasn't lying on a tropical beach. The RV. The sofa bed. *Mark.*

After she'd fallen asleep, she must have moved into his arms. The sedation of sleep dropped away in an instant and everything came into focus. A broad expanse of chest. The hard lines of a muscular arm, draped over her back. Her leg, oh Lord, her leg curled across his—

Claire bolted upright. When she did, her leg grazed Mark's midsection. It didn't take a genius to realize *he'd* been dreaming about something *other* than beaches.

About her?

Just as quickly as the thought came, Claire dismissed it. She drew the blanket to her chest and settled against her pillow. The afghan wasn't big enough for two and the movement pulled it off Mark. Hastily, she bent forward to cover him.

She hesitated. Her gaze took in the ridges of muscle along his stomach, the dark line of hair that trailed down to the waistband of his boxers, the lean, defined thighs—

"See something you like?"

Claire gasped, jerked back. "No, I was just...just..." Her mouth refused to cooperate with her brain.

"Admit it. You were checking me out."

"I was not!" She sounded about as mature as a toddler.

Mark rolled onto his side and propped his head on his hand. "Yeah. I believe that." He grinned and she felt as if he could see right through her, even in the dark.

"I was putting a blanket over you. You looked cold." She could hear the high, defensive pitch in her voice. What was it about this man that pushed her buttons?

He chuckled. "I tried that line earlier. Did *you* buy it?"

She smiled. "No."

"Come on. We're two healthy adults. In bed together. It's inevitable that we might sneak a peek." His grin turned into a Cheshire-cat smile. "Or cop a feel."

"I did no such thing!"

"That wasn't your leg draped over my—" he gestured toward his waist.

"I didn't do that because of you." She raised her chin a notch and dared him to defy her answer. "I was dreaming about George Clooney."

He snorted. "Right. You weren't thinking about me at all?"

Before she could reply, he moved to her side, raising himself over her and planting his hands on either side of her head. His mouth was inches from hers. With the smallest of efforts, she could lean forward and kiss him. She wanted to, oh how she wanted to. Since their alliance earlier today and the quiet conversation they'd had before drifting off to sleep, something had shifted between them, something monumental. She wondered about his motives for asking Nancy to dinner…had it been to make her jealous? In Mark's eyes, she was sure she read interest. Interest in her, no one else.

A flutter of happiness ran through her. She should have been annoyed or frustrated—anything but happy that

Mark found her interesting. That he might have been thinking about her as more than the girl down the street.

"You know," Mark began, "an hour ago, when we were talking, all I could think about was us being friends."

"Yeah. Me, too." Although, to be honest, thoughts of friendship were pretty far away right now.

"I didn't plan to take advantage of being in bed with you."

She swallowed. "That's good to know."

"But all that changed when I went back to sleep. In my dreams, Claire, you were pretty insistent on wanting much more than friendship." A teasing grin played at his lips. "I can control what happens when I'm awake, but I have no control over my dreams. Or what you do to me in them."

"Me neither." He was so close. An hour ago, that closeness had meant comfort, security. But now, the air had changed and his proximity meant something different altogether. Something she wanted much more than she was willing to admit.

He traced along her jaw with his index finger. Tendrils of heat snaked through her body, tightening and tingling. In the dark, his eyes almost glowed and the heat between them became palpable. "You've grown up, Claire."

"Kids tend to do that."

"Not everyone grows up as nicely as you do." His voice was husky and low. Sexy.

"You...you didn't do so bad." Her usual sardonic tongue had deserted her.

"I don't want to talk about me. In fact, I don't want to talk at all. I think we did plenty of that already." His hand cupped the side of her face, his thumb tracing a slow semicircle along her cheek. "Don't you agree?"

She breathed the word. "Yes."

"Good." Then Mark leaned forward and kissed her.

The movement caught her off guard and threw her senses into immediate overload. Since they'd boarded the RV, she had wondered, for brief moments, what it would be like to kiss Mark.

She hadn't expected this.

His mouth didn't just touch hers—it conquered. In one deft movement, he managed to wipe away all the reasons she'd thought it was a bad idea to get close to him. His tongue darted in against hers, teasing her, making her arch against him.

Claire wrapped her arms around Mark's neck and drew him down to the bed—to her. He pressed along her length. The silk of his boxers tickled along her thighs, the planes of his chest crushed to her breasts, escalating her desire.

His kiss was tempestuous, tossing and turning her emotions like a winter storm. Heated and fierce, yet tender and reverent, all at once. His mouth slid over hers, moist and hot, nipping, insistent, asking for all she had.

She gave him what he wanted—what she wanted—with a ferocity that surprised her. It was as if a switch had been turned on in her brain, one that changed all the dynamics between them.

She had thought he was like every other man she'd ever known. In the last few days, he had shown her that he wasn't. He'd exposed a vulnerable side to himself, opening the door to the true Mark, a man who had more dimensions than she'd thought.

That he could kiss this well was a double bonus. One that sent her emotions soaring into a stratosphere she'd never visited before. She gripped him, holding on as if he was a life preserver in an ocean teeming with mistakes and lonely nights. He moaned and tightened against her, his touch an echo of hers.

Mark's hands danced down her sides, slipping over the curves of her hips. She shifted against him, enjoying the feeling of power when he groaned. Claire pressed her legs to his, asking with her body for more. She nipped his lower lip with her teeth and he moved to take her ferociously in his arms again, crushing her body to his, making no secret of how much he wanted her.

Coherent thought left her. The powerful magnetism between them built in intensity, cresting and rolling like an ocean tide rushing into the beach. His hands moved to her chest, cupping her breasts through the soft cotton of her shirt.

When his fingers brushed the sensitive tips, reality slammed into her like a brick wall. Claire jolted out of his arms and scrambled to her feet, shoving her shirt down. "We can't do this."

Mark blinked at her. "Can't do what?"

"This…" she gestured at the bed, at him, at herself. Her heart still hammered in her chest, her pulse roared in her ears. "I can't get involved with you. Not like that."

"And what makes you think it's going to go much further?"

She snorted. "Doesn't it always?"

Mark got to his feet and moved toward her, cupping her face with his hands. In the dark, his eyes seemed to bore into hers. "I want you. More than you know. But that doesn't mean the only thing I want is to sleep with you. With any other woman… Well, you aren't every other woman." He swallowed, began again. "I don't want us to rush into anything, either. I care about you too much. We're adults and presumably smart enough to know there are…ramifications for doing this."

Emotion tumbled through Claire's heart. No man had ever said that, no one had ever thought about her beyond what her body could give. No one. Except Mark. "You're the last person I'd expect to say something like that."

He drew his fingers along her jaw in a light, tender caress. "Maybe you don't know me as well as you thought." He leaned forward, brushing her lips with his own, a kiss so close to chaste that it touched Claire more than anything she'd ever received. "I'm not every other man, Claire. I'm not eighteen and breaking someone's heart on prom night. I've changed, grown up. Why won't you trust me?"

She didn't answer. The reasons were all on the tip of her tongue, but for some reason, her mouth wouldn't cooperate.

"I was an idiot." Mark traced the outline of her lips, a simple movement that sent waves of tingles through her. "I never should have asked Nancy out. I was just trying to make you—"

"Jealous?" she supplied.

"Yeah." He shook his head. "It's like I was twelve years old again and you were turning me down for the Spring Fling."

"I don't remember doing that."

"I do. You were always telling me to bug off when we were kids." He smiled. "You drove me crazy. But at the same time, I wanted nothing more than to kiss you."

"Kiss me?" All she could do was parrot his words. His touch, and the things he was saying, had her mind racing off into new, unexplored territory.

"Whenever I get near you, I feel like I'm twelve again. I never manage to say or do the right thing."

She couldn't resist a smile. "Do I make you nervous?"

"No. You make me try harder." His hand lingered on her chin. "I think that's a good thing. Don't you?"

Before she could answer—or deal with the effect his words were having on her heart—the bed in the cab above them began to squeak-squeak-squeak again. Claire pulled away from Mark, the magical spell broken.

"Seems we're not the only ones having fun," he whispered.

"You call...what we were just doing," she gestured for the words she didn't have, "having fun?"

"Oh yeah." He brushed a lock of hair off her face and tucked it behind her ear. The tenderness of the movement brought a surprising sting to her eyes.

For so many years, Mark had been the boy next door. The cliché of it all didn't go unnoticed by Claire. These few days locked together on the RV had forced her to look at him with new eyes. She'd seen how much he'd grown up, how much he'd changed. He'd become a man that she could depend on, talk to...maybe even love.

Love? Where had that word come from? Love most certainly did not figure into her plans. No, not at all. But as she glanced back at Mark, she began to wonder...what if it did?

The room was suddenly filled with harsh white light. Mark and Claire broke apart, both blinking from the glare.

Millie stood there, knitting needles raised in her right hand like a policeman's nightstick. "You should be ashamed of yourselves," she yelled in Roger and Jessica's direction.

Roger stuck his head out from behind the curtains closing in their "bedroom." "Give us a break. We just got married."

"That's what a hotel room is for." She wagged the

needles at him. "So you can do *that* in private. There's
no need to wake up the entire house with your antics."

"What the hell is going on?" Danny asked with a
sleepy yawn. When no one answered, he buried his face
into the chair and shielded his head from the light.

"You can't tell us what to do," Roger said. "Jessica's
my wife. If I want to do 'antics' with her, I will."

Millie parked her fists on her hips. "Once Nancy Lewis
hears about it, you'll be off this RV before you can say
'I need a cigarette.'"

Claire looked at Mark and bit her lip to keep from
laughing. She saw a mirroring smirk on his face.

Millie plopped into the recliner, grabbed her knitting
from behind the seat, but didn't take out any yarn. She
cast a sour look at the cab bed, then crossed her arms and
knitting needles across her chest like an Egyptian pharaoh.
"I'll stay right here and keep an eye on you kids."

Roger let out a few loud and vulgar curses that made
Millie purse her lips tighter. "Come on, Jessica. We're
outta here."

Claire could hear them wrangling into clothes, then
they came down from the bed and marched past Millie.
Jessica was crying and asking Roger to reconsider. But
his libido must have been stronger than his need for an
RV, because he kept right on moving until he'd reached
the back bedroom, retrieved their luggage, then left the
RV, slamming the door behind him.

Millie ignored the entire theatrical departure. She pulled
out her yarn from the bag and started in on another afghan. Click, clack. Click, clack.

Claire and Mark settled back against the bed, resuming
their earlier perches on the edge. The mood between them
had cooled, particularly under the watchful eye of Millie.

For the first time since boarding the motor home, Claire

felt gratitude for Millie's presence. She and her knitting needles had given Claire a respite from the confusing emotions rushing through her.

Had she just been thinking about dating Mark? A man well known for his string of girlfriends and lack of commitment to anything? He'd said he changed. But he'd also asked another woman to dinner earlier today.

Thank God for Millie. She'd just headed off one more in a long line of mistakes made when Claire believed the whispers of a man in bed.

Chapter Nine

Luke,

I haven't slept a hell of a lot lately, and no, I won't tell you why. Suffice to say just having Claire in the same room makes it tough to concentrate on much of anything. That grandmother, Millie, knitted all night, watching us like a hawk. I've been working most of the early morning, which is probably the smartest thing right now. Give Em a hug for me.

Mark

Mark pressed Send, then opened up the file for his training program proposal. He scrolled through it and had to admit the whole thing had come together nicely. He knew two former clients of his and Luke's who had expressed interest in such a program last year, but at the time, the whole thing had been just an idea, not anything concrete. Now he actually had something to offer. With a whispered prayer, Mark composed an e-mail to each of them and sent the proposal off into cyberspace.

He sat back and worked the kinks out of his neck before shutting down the laptop and tucking it into his bag. Across the room, he noticed Millie had finally fallen asleep. She was snoring, too, almost the same hock-hocking sound as Lester. God forbid Claire ever snored like that when she was his wife—

His wife? Since when had he started thinking of Claire as a possible wife? Mark glanced at her. She hugged her side of the bed, her back to him. Her hair was spread out like a golden cloud and the blanket had slipped down again to her hips. As he looked at her, he realized the thought had been in his head almost since the competition had started.

Somewhere along the path between screwing up his life and Luke's, Mark had decided to change from playboy to family man. Growing up meant realizing what was really important, what would complete his life—settling down, remaining in one place, with one woman. Out of all the women he had dated, he couldn't think of a single one he'd wanted to stay with for more than a few days.

Except Claire. All he could think of was how much he wanted her today and the next day and the next, on down for the years of his life. He couldn't imagine not being with her, seeing her smile, hearing her laugh and laughing back at her well-aimed jabs, for the rest of forever.

Mark Dole, avowed bachelor, was falling in love.

As if called by telepathy, Claire rolled over and faced him. "Hey," she said, her voice still husky with sleep.

"Hey yourself."

She got to her feet, tugging down her shirt as she did, and padded into the kitchen. The long T-shirt extended past her thighs, but left plenty of bare leg exposed, much to Mark's enjoyment. Even in the morning, with her face bare of makeup, Claire looked beautiful. The natural radiance of her features seemed more brilliant in the soft interior light.

"There's coffee." Mark rose, crossed to the counter and slipped the pot from the brewer. "Sit down. I'll get you a cup."

"Thanks." She settled onto the bench seat, then turned and raised two fingers. "Can you put in two—"

"Sugars and a splash of cream," he finished. A look of surprise filled her face. "I pay attention, Claire."

"I…I'm flattered. No one has ever learned how I like my coffee."

"I told you, I'm not like the other guys you've known."

"Maybe not," she conceded. She tucked her legs beneath her and ran a hand through her hair, displacing the waves of gold. Mark jerked himself back to his task before he spilled coffee down the front of his sweats.

He sat the cup before her, taking the opposite seat. "You know…" He let out a deep breath before testing the waters with words he'd never said before. "It's too bad we aren't married."

Claire let out a cough that sounded as though she was choking. "Married?"

"If we were married, we could both win." He grinned, softening the seriousness of his words. Anything to erase the look of panic in Claire's eyes. "And then we'd ride happily into the sunset."

She shook her head. "Marriage is not part of my dream."

He took a sip of coffee. The warm liquid slid to the pit of his stomach with a hefty flavoring of disappointment. "Why not?"

"Because it would tie me right back down to this town." She wrapped her hands around her mug. "I made that mistake once. I'm not doing it again. I haven't lived *my* life yet. I've just lived the one I was stuck with because I made some dumb choices."

"With a guy?"

She nodded and drank some coffee before answering. "My biggest mistake was named Travis. We were in *love*," she drew out the word with sarcasm. Mark remembered hearing about her dating Travis and had heard Jenny complaining about Claire's choice. "Or, at least, I was. He told me we were engaged, but he never bothered with a ring, so basically what it boiled down to was one big facade of loving bliss."

"But why would you get involved with him?"

She let out a sigh. "I can't tell you how awful it was living with Abe. He…he didn't give a damn about me and never noticed me, unless the floor needed to be mopped or the fridge was empty." She shook her head. "When I was eighteen, all I wanted to do was get away from that. So I fell in love with the first thing in jeans, believed every word he said and moved in with him." She let out a breath that seemed to steady her, then drank again from the mug. "We lived together for three years while he strung me along, making one promise after another. He worked in the steel mill, just like his dad and his brothers and his uncles…you get the picture."

"What about you?"

"I took a job at Flo's as a shampooer. Then I went to beauty school. I figured it would be a good career to fall back on, if the cooking thing didn't work out. Travis said our situation was temporary, until we had enough money to get a van and leave town." She snorted. "He got the van. And forgot to take me. He went off to Nashville, to make it big, I guess. At least he left me a note. And a lease and a rack of charges on my credit card.'' Her smile was sardonic. ''Some mementos, huh?''

''What about after he left? Why not get out of town then?''

She stared at a spot past him for a few seconds. ''I should have. But I didn't. Abe got hurt in a bar fight and I ended up taking care of him. I know, brand me stupid, but I felt like I owed him something. My mother had loved him, and I suppose I could understand that. When he was sober, he was funny and a man who can make you smile is easy to forgive.'' She closed her eyes and turned away. ''Anyway, by the time Abe was well again, it just seemed easier to stay in Mercy. I had a job, I had a house I was renting. I told myself that's all I needed.''

''And now?''

''Now I've finally got my shot. I'm not backing down this time. I gave my notice at Flo's before I got on the RV. Win or lose, I still have to start over again.''

''That's a pretty gutsy move.''

She shook her head and he saw the smudges of fear in her eyes. ''Not gutsy, Mark. Desperate.'' She got to her feet, crossed to the counter and poured another cup of coffee. But instead of returning, she lingered by the pot, twirling a spoonful of sugar into her mug.

''What's in California that you don't have here?''

''Family.'' She said the word so softly, he had to strain to catch it. She took in a breath, let it out, then turned to face him, all Claire again. ''Anyway, it's time I started my life. I've been living here for twenty-eight years, always because of someone else. First Travis, then Abe. Every man I've ever known has only wanted me for housekeeping or income.'' She snorted. ''It's my turn now. I'm not going to let anyone sidetrack me.''

Mark rose and moved to her side. He laid a hand on hers. "You can have all that with a man, too. If he loves you, he'll want you to go for your dreams."

She pulled away. "Yeah, and have him leave me after I've gone and fallen in love again, like an idiot?"

"Real love doesn't mean you're an idiot, Claire." He turned her to face him. In her eyes, he saw a glimmer of tears. "Maybe what you felt with Travis wasn't real."

She swallowed. "Since when did you become an expert?" But her words lacked the usual sarcasm.

He was about to say "Just now," but stopped himself. Claire wanted very simple things in life. The chance to see if she could succeed or fail on her own. Mark could appreciate that. He wanted much the same thing for himself. Hadn't he wondered all these years if he could make it on his own, without Luke's help? Achieve things on his own merit? Claire hadn't had that chance yet and if he pushed her right now to marry him, he'd end up putting her back into the very box she was trying to escape. So instead of saying what was in his heart, he lied. "I'm not an expert, Claire. I don't know much about love at all."

Before she could respond—or worse, agree—he retreated. He grabbed his notebook, took a seat up front and commandeered the remote out of Danny's sleepy grip. The television droned while he attempted to work. He didn't get a damned thing written.

All he did was stare out the window and figure as far as screw-ups went, his proposal of marriage topped the list.

After Mark left, Claire dumped her coffee down the kitchen sink drain. The gourmet blend suddenly tasted bitter. Then she escaped to the bathroom, trying not to think about what had just transpired. But still, the conversation with Mark replayed itself again and again in her mind. In some roundabout way, had he just asked her to marry him?

She closed her eyes and let the hot shower trickle down her face. Marriage to Mark. A crazy idea, to be sure. But even as she thought it, the images of domesticity, of life together, flashed through her mind. Of happy smiles and kisses at the door, of Chinese take-out in bed and cuddles on the couch.

She shook her head, dispelling the images. Mark wasn't the kind of guy to get married. Was he?

Could he…love her?

He'd seemed awfully hurt when she'd asked him what made him an expert on the subject of love. She turned, letting the shower hit her shoulders and back. When she opened her eyes and faced the white stall walls, pictures of Mark flashed before her eyes.

His simple massage on her neck, deft fingers seeking only to soothe, not seduce.

His kiss, so ferocious in intensity, but so layered with reverence, as if she were a porcelain doll in his arms.

And on top of it all, he knew exactly how she took her coffee.

Sharp tears sprung in her eyes. Her heart began to hammer in her chest, her pulse skittering with newfound realizations. When had a man ever cared enough about her to pay attention?

And when had she ever been so moved by such a simple gesture?

Claire shook herself. Getting involved with Mark right now would be crazy. She had plans. Dreams. He wasn't a part of that. He couldn't be. In the end, he'd be like everyone else in her life—her mother, Travis, even Abe—and leave.

Claire reminded herself that she needed no one. She was severing her ties here. And those ties included Mark Dole.

Unfortunately, he was impossible to escape. As soon as she emerged from the bathroom, she saw him sitting in the kitchen with the others. He had changed into a deep-blue golf shirt and a pair of jeans. The soft cotton hugged his frame, the blue setting off his eyes. He'd left the top button undone and she could see the hollow of his neck.

She ducked back against the wall and closed her eyes. What would it be like to kiss him there? To run her hands over the softness of his shirt, to hold him again, just as she had last night? To let those kisses take them further and finally—

She opened her eyes before her thoughts could go any further. She was moving on, getting out of this town. A man didn't fit into the equation.

Claire rounded the corner and entered the kitchen. The four at the table were eating breakfast in almost total silence. Over the days, conversation had dropped off between everyone, even Millie and Lester. It occurred to Claire as she dished up her own bowl of cereal that the group had settled into life as old marrieds, with nothing but the daily news as verbal exchange.

Danny polished off a bowl of corn flakes and bananas, got to his feet and stretched. "Well, I'm off."

"Off?" Lester said.

"I'm done. I'm leaving."

Everyone blinked at him in surprise. "Just like that?" Millie asked.

"Yeah. My vacation's over."

"*This* was your vacation?" Claire said.

"The bus had a great TV and mine was broken." He shrugged. "I wanted to catch the end of the Cowboys season and this seemed like a good plan. But now, I gotta get back to work.''

"You have a *job?*" Millie's jaw nearly touched the floor.

"Yeah. Sort of. I work at the gas station sometimes. I'm a cleanup guy. Someone makes a mess, I clean it up.''

Millie looked pointedly at his cereal bowl, milk slopped all over the table, crumbs of corn flakes scattered here and there from when he poured his breakfast. "Really?"

"Yeah. It's a crappy job, but it pays enough to live. Well, to live at home with my mom.'' He shrugged again, then gave them all a wave. "It's been real, but I have to go.''

And just like that, Danny was gone, clutching his paper bag of belongings and whistling as he walked through the mall toward the exit. The four of them took seats at the table, gaping at each other.

"*That* was his vacation?" Millie said.

"One more down," Claire wrote in her journal after breakfast.

If I could just figure out a way to get rid of Millie and Lester... Still, there's Mark. He has a good reason for wanting the RV, but not one as important as mine. I wish I could just close my eyes and wake up in California.

And then Claire did close her eyes. The tears that had threatened all morning spilled over. She ached with need for her father—for family. For belonging. For someone who loved her just because.

There was a knock at the door to the bedroom and Claire sat up sharply, swiping away the tears. "Yeah?"

"You decent?" Mark's voice.

"Yeah."

He came in, took one look at her and shut the door. He crossed to the bed, taking her into his arms. The tears started in earnest again, pouring from her with a mixture of relief and need. She clutched at Mark, drawing comfort from his presence. For the first time in her life, Claire Richards relied on someone else for strength. And, she realized from somewhere deep inside, it didn't feel bad or weak or stupid at all. In Mark's arms, it felt right.

When she was done crying, she pulled back and wiped her face with her hand. "I'm sorry. I…"

"Shhh…" He grabbed a tissue from a box on the nightstand and dabbed away the tears. "You don't have to explain."

"Yeah, I do. Considering I ruined your shirt, the least I can do is tell you why." She let out a weak laugh and ran her hand down the wet spot on the front of his shirt. The touch of him beneath her palm felt solid, reassuring. Dependable. How she needed to depend on someone else, if only for five minutes. "I want to win the RV so I can go see my father."

"Abe? I thought he died."

"He did. I meant my real father. I found him a few weeks ago. Or rather, I shocked him by telling him he had a daughter. All these years, he'd never known he had a child." She sighed.

"How is that possible?"

"When Abe died, I had to sell the house. In the attic, I found a box of my mother's things that I'd never known existed. I found a journal and in it, there was a copy of my birth certificate with his name on it and some letters. Love letters. I hired a private investigator, gave him what little information I had, and within a few weeks, they'd found him. My father was completely surprised when I contacted him last month. He'd had no idea.''

"Wow. That's unbelievable," Mark said. "But why would your mother not tell him about you?"

She took a breath, then let out the story that had been a secret for too many years. "When she was seventeen, she went to spend the summer on her uncle's horse farm in Kentucky. She loved horses and loved to ride. She met my father there. He was the son of the neighbors. He'd just joined the army and was leaving at the end of the summer for basic training. He was several years older than her. When her parents found out about this older guy, who was seemingly just out for a summer fling, they were furious. They pressured her to end it, so she wrote him a 'Dear John' letter while he was in basic training and broke it off. She found out she was pregnant afterwards. Her parents, worried about a scandal, sent her back to the farm for her senior year."

"And you were such a cute baby, your mother had to keep you?" The teasing brought a smile to Claire's face.

"When I was born, my grandparents let her move back home. On two conditions. She was never to contact my father again and she had to finish high school. She did that, but then she married Abe the day after graduation. So in the end, all their rules didn't keep her from making a bad choice for a husband." Claire let out a sigh. "Everyone in town always assumed Abe was my father because she married him so soon after she had me."

"Wow. She never talked to your dad again?"

"No. He never knew about me, or any of this, until I called him. Shocked the hell out of him." She swiped at her eyes again. "I'm twenty-eight years old and I've never met my own father."

"He's at least fifty and he's never met his own daughter."

"True." Claire sighed. "I wonder what he looks like, if he's taller than me, if we have the same eyes. All that stuff."

"So why doesn't he just hop on a plane and come out here? Or why don't you go visit him?"

"It's not that easy." She swallowed. "He's sick."

"Sick?"

"Cancer." She exhaled the word like it was a bag of stones. "Lung cancer, to be precise. How ironic that he's dying of the same big C word that killed my mother. Hers was ovarian and it took her so young, before I had much time with her. I guess that's why I'm so afraid I'm going to lose him before I get a chance to meet him."

Claire sucked in a breath as if she was trying very hard not to cry. Mark reached out, took her hand in his and gave it a squeeze. A weak version of her smile flitted across her face.

Mark realized how lucky he'd been to grow up with a mother and a father, both still alive and still together. He'd known Claire had had a hard-knocks life, but had never known the details. Claire was the type to keep these things to herself, to put on a devil-may-care smile and pretend everything was fine.

He tucked an errant lock of hair behind her ear, letting his hand linger against her cheek. "Can't they do anything?"

"They are. He's got a round of chemo coming up soon because the surgery and the radiation didn't get it all. The doctor doesn't want him traveling too far before the chemo and not at all once it starts. I wanted to win this so I could—" she cut herself off. "It sounds corny."

"Tell me."

She bit her lip, then finished. ''I wanted to win this so I could take my dad on a trip. I've never met him, never had more than a few phone conversations with him. I thought if we spent a week driving around California, we could really get to know each other. No interruptions, no other people. No hospital rooms and nurses. Just me and my dad.''

Suddenly, the Survive and Drive contest took on layers of meaning it hadn't had before. Claire didn't want to win the RV for some superfluous reason like the others, she wanted it to give her the one thing she'd never had—a chance at a family.

Mark knew that ache for someone who would complete his soul. In the last few days, he'd learned an awful lot about wanting someone who seemed a thousand miles away. He could feel Claire's longing, could hear her pain, her need.

''That's not corny at all,'' he said softly.

''Sure it is.'' She let out a snort. ''I've got this big Oprah moment in my head, as if I can drive out there, take him on a vacation, wipe away three decades in a week, and oh, on the way, pick up the magic cure somewhere in the Rockies. He's getting so bad, though, that by the time I get there—'' She sucked in a breath, ''it will probably be too late.'' Her voice cracked.

Mark drew Claire against him again. He didn't ponder how beautiful Claire was, how this was an opportunity to get much more than a hug. Any other day, with any other woman, that would have been Mark's sole motivation. But not this time. He didn't think about anything but the sadness lacing her words together and how much she needed someone to lean on, to help her.

Six days ago, nothing had seemed more important than winning the motor home, driving it to California and selling it to fund the new start for Luke and himself. He'd had a single mission—to atone for his mistakes. When he'd boarded the RV, he hadn't imagined anything becoming more important than that.

And then along came Claire. Her need was simple. Primal. To find the family she'd never known. Really, the family she'd never had, considering how young she'd been when her mother had died. He couldn't imagine what it was like to be so alone, to have no siblings, no parents, no history of pillow fights and Christmas Days. Yet she'd carried that load so well, anyone who looked at her would never suspect she'd pretty much raised herself. No wonder she'd never gotten close to people. Everyone she'd ever loved had pretty much abandoned her.

He didn't have the heart to let Claire flounder alone, while he walked away with the one thing she needed most.

"You'll win the RV," he said, knowing he had just compounded his own problems, but no longer caring about himself. He closed his eyes and laid his chin on top of her head. "I'll make sure of it."

"Mark, no. You have your own reasons for needing it—"

"They don't matter, Claire. Yours is more important."

"But still, you can't guarantee I'll win it."

"For you, Claire, sure I can." He cupped her face with his palm and tipped it until she was looking at him. "I'm a hero, remember? I can do anything."

A half hour later, Claire and Mark exited the bedroom. The whole time, she'd talked about her father. It felt as if she'd just crawled out of a deep well. Her head was clearer, her heart lighter, and although her father was as sick and as far away as he'd been this morning, reaching him in time suddenly seemed like a very real possibility.

Mark's promise had given her the first ray of hope she'd felt in a long, long time. She started to tell him how grateful she was when there was a knock at the door. Before anyone could answer it, James Kent and his camera crew barged inside.

"Good morning, everyone! We're here to catch some footage of life in the motor home." He turned to the cameraman behind him. "Make sure you get shots of everyone behaving naturally," he said. "Make it real."

"Oh no, you don't!" Millie scrambled out from the kitchen table. "I don't have my face on yet." She dashed past Claire and Mark, slamming the bedroom door behind her.

Claire's face was bare, too, but with James Kent practically on top of them, she saw no sense in running for the bathroom like a prom queen who'd spilled punch on her dress.

This time, there were three cameras. Once inside, the cameramen fanned out, each taking a section. They perched on a chair, against the wall and beside the refrigerator. The silent, black, oversized eyes of the cameras watched every move they made. It was a freaky feeling and Claire wished again she'd read the fine print before signing on the dotted line.

No one moved or said anything. "Well, go on. Go about your day," James said, shooing at them. "Act natural."

Natural? Impossible. Standing there like the village idiot wouldn't be smart, either, though. Claire moved first, cleaning up the rest of the dishes and making a production out of washing the counter. Mark appeared at her side, took up a dishtowel and began to dry. "I have an idea," he whispered.

"If it gets those cameras out of my face, I'm interested."

"Follow my lead. We'll have Millie and Lester—and the Lawford News—off in no time." He tossed the towel onto the counter and crossed to James Kent.

Chapter Ten

Mark swallowed hard and settled into the armchair. Confession was good for the soul, they said. He hoped that was true and that, through it he'd be able to rebuild his own soul. After the last few days, it seemed even more imperative, especially now that he'd seen the possibility of what he could have with Claire.

Before he'd returned to Mercy with Luke, he'd realized he didn't like the man who looked back at him in the mirror. Sitting down with the reporter and spilling the truth about his past was the first step in erasing that image, and, he hoped, the start of building a new one.

He glanced at Claire. It was enough to double his resolve.

"This is James Kent with Ten-Spot News. I'm here with Mark Dole, who was given the key to the city by the Mayor of Lawford almost twenty years ago for his dramatic rescue of another boy. Ever since, Mr. Dole has been the poster child of a hero." James cocked his head, waited a dramatic pause. "Today, however, he's here to tell a very different story." He turned and thrust the microphone into Mark's face. "Tell me about that day, Mr. Dole."

Mark folded his hands together, then began the story he'd told Claire the night before. He didn't gloss over the truth, he just laid the facts on the table and left them to be judged on their own merit.

"That's quite the secret to keep," James said when Mark was done. He signaled to the cameraman to shut off the equipment.

"Yeah, it was."

James studied him. "You seem almost...*glad* to have the truth out."

"You know, I am. To have something like this hanging on your conscience for all these years...when it's gone, it's like you've lost a hundred pounds in five minutes."

"But in the end, you did rescue that boy. He owes his life to you."

"I wouldn't say that. It could have easily gone the other way." Mark fiddled with the piping on the arm of the chair. "I'm just thankful it had a happy ending."

"The world could use a few more of those." Then James did a surprising thing. He stuck out his hand. Mark hesitated a fraction of a second before accepting. The two men shook. "I admire you for coming forward with your story, Mr. Dole. You gave me a lot more than the story I thought I was looking for. Guess it's time I listened more often instead of presuming the truth." A sheepish smile crossed his face. "Thank you."

The reporter stepped back and signaled to the trio of cameramen. The four huddled for a moment, conferring and talking about time left on the tape, angles and lighting. Two crew members left. James and one cameraman stayed.

The feeling of freedom fluttered in Mark's veins. He'd released one albatross from his neck. The truth about the past was finally public. Hercules had been reduced to a mortal again. And it felt damned good.

He owed one more person an explanation—Luke. Then Mark would truly be standing on his own two feet, to succeed or fail on his own merit. He'd be ready to embark on the future he'd been dreaming of. A future with Claire.

She sat in the kitchen, watching him, a confused look on her face. Her hair had escaped its ponytail and hung in loose tendrils around her neck. She wasn't perfect. She was beautiful. His arms ached to hold her, to take her back to that sofa bed, to what they'd had last night before real life had intruded.

He realized at that moment, looking at the woman he had known nearly all his life, that he wasn't just falling in love with her. Hell, he'd already done that a long time ago. No, now it was much more. He loved her. Irrevocably. He couldn't imagine going one day without her.

He crossed to Claire and settled into one of the barstools.

"Why did you tell him all of that?" Claire asked.

"Two reasons. One, I made a deal with our friend Mr. Kent."

"A deal?"

"I gave him what he wanted most—a juicy story that he can splash all over the news—in exchange for him doing what he does best." Mark smiled. "Harass people."

Claire raised her hands, as if warding him off. "Don't tell me he's going to be here more than he already is."

"Oh, he will be. He'll practically be moving in, but he won't bother you or me. His target is—"

"Millie," Claire finished in a whisper, with a nod of

understanding. She smiled at him and it zinged his heart. "You are a crafty one, Mr. Dole."

"Nothing you and I did was making Millie budge. I suppose we could have driven her crazy by making wild love on the kitchen table, but…" Mark cast a look over his shoulder in Millie's direction. "I'm a little afraid of those needles."

Claire laughed and tried, in vain, to block the image of doing exactly that from her mind. As much as her brain told her not to get involved with Mark, her body had very different plans. The simmering attraction between them had reached a full boil last night. Claire felt it in the heat of Mark's gaze, in the jolt of electricity in his touch.

"So," she said, clearing her throat before all those feelings could show, "what is Mr. Kent going to do?"

"Drive her nuts. Dog her every move. Catch her without her face on. In general, make life so miserable, she leaves."

"Why would he do that? A knitting grandma isn't exactly exciting."

"No, but he's hoping she'll blow up at him and give him some footage of a raging senior citizen. He said that makes good TV. Besides, he said it's a slow news day and his only assignment for today is the RV. So, bugging Millie keeps him earning his paycheck."

"The man is a creep."

"He may have one or two redeeming qualities," Mark replied. "Either way, he's a creep who will, I hope, get Millie and Lester off the RV. And then, it's yours."

"Mark, really, you don't have to—"

"Let me do this for you." Mark let out a breath and looked away. "I haven't done too many things in my life I'm proud of. I'm not too old to start over again, to try and be the person I should have been that day on the ice, but I'm going to try.''

''But what about—'' Claire cut off her sentence when the bedroom door opened and Millie emerged, freshly made up and dressed in a gray twin set and slacks. True to his word, James Kent signaled to his cameraman to train the lens on her. She ignored them and went to her knitting.

At first, Millie seemed to enjoy the attention. But after a half hour of James, she clearly wasn't having fun. She flashed several annoyed looks at James, but managed to keep her cool. She just knitted away, the click-clacking now a furious sound.

Mark got to his feet. ''I better hop in the shower while there's still some water left.'' He paused, a question in his eyes. ''The cookies are long gone…''

Claire laughed. ''My shampoo and soap are in the cabinet under the sink. Enjoy.''

''I definitely will.'' He placed a quick kiss on her lips. Too short. Too little. Later…maybe there'd be more.

True to his word, James tracked Millie's every move, practically tripping over her in his effort to get the story. When she got up to get a drink of water, he and his camera followed. When she started making up Lester's morning shake, James was right there, asking about the ingredients and quizzing Millie on their health benefits.

As soon as Mark exited the bathroom, Millie barreled full-speed for the door and slipped inside. James turned to Lester, cornering him on the couch. Lester, however, was more than content to talk about the grandkids and his woodworking hobby. For twenty minutes, he chatted with the reporter, regaling him with tales of the latest escapades of the grandkids.

Claire and Mark settled themselves at the kitchen table,

ostensibly playing gin rummy, but really watching for a blowup. When Millie finally exited the bathroom, James was back in her face, quizzing her about her children and her knitting.

It took until after lunch before the strain began to show in Millie's face. Claire almost felt sorry, then remembered the knitting needles and decided Millie had sown enough discontent to reap a little for herself.

"Young man, don't you have a fire or a bank robbery to cover?" Millie sputtered after the black eye of the cameras had watched her work on an afghan for twenty minutes. She laid her knitting in her lap, halfway through a row of green stitches. Claire could see the pattern of the row was irregular, as if the attention of the cameras had disrupted her knit-one, purl-two.

"Not right now," James said. His cell phone rang. He answered it, said a few words, then hung up. "How's that for irony? That was my producer. The Mayor of Lawford is announcing his retirement at two. I need to cover it. Sorry." Five minutes later, the reporter was gone.

And there were still four people on the RV. Claire dropped her head into her hands and let out a sigh.

"Don't worry," Mark said, taking the seat beside her in the dinette. "It'll work out."

"How?" Disappointment shot through her. "Maybe I can ask Nancy to get us a cattle prod on her next grocery trip."

Mark laughed. He laid a hand over Claire's and gave it a squeeze. The connection provided the brief boost of reassurance she needed. Ignoring her mind's warnings, Claire leaned against Mark's shoulder and snuggled close. It felt so good to ease into Mark, so right.

"Well," Millie said, clearing her throat as she entered the kitchen. "I'm glad that's over."

Lester toddled out of the bathroom and into the kitchen. He opened the refrigerator and began rummaging through the shelves.

"Lester, dear?" Millie said. Her husband looked up. "It's time for your afternoon shake."

Lester made a face and slammed the door shut. "Nope."

"Why it's twelve-thirty, dear. Let me just—" she started to bustle past him but he stopped her.

"I said no. I'm not drinking that anymore. I'd rather die ten years sooner than have one more of those damned things." He straightened and Millie took a step back. "And another thing, Millicent." He wagged a finger at her.

"What?"

"I don't want a damned RV. We don't even like Florida. Too hot. Too many bugs. Why you ever talked me into this competition, I'll never know." He shook his head. "I'm tired of being retired. It's boring as hell. I can't sit around all day and watch your stories and play canasta. I need to be busy." He turned to Mark. "You've taught me something, young man."

"Me?" Mark answered.

"Over the days, I saw how fired up you got whenever you were working on that computer. I used to feel that way myself, back when I had my cleaning business. I miss that feeling." Lester laid a hand on Mark's shoulder. "Whatever you do with your life, don't forget the things that spur you out of bed in the morning. That's what makes for a long life. Not naps and power shakes." He grimaced.

"But—but—what about the RV?" Millie said.

"We're getting off this land boat, Millicent. I may be retired, but I'm not spending the rest of my life cooped up in an overgrown car. First, we're going to go on an adventure. Maybe a safari. Or a trip around Europe. And then, when we get back home, I'm going to make a business out of that woodworking I've been doing.'' He gave her a determined nod.

"A safari? Europe? Oh, how wonderful!'' Millie put her arms around him. "Truth be told, I didn't want the RV, either. I thought you wanted it.'' She gave him a squeeze. "I'm so happy to see you back to being yourself, Lester.''

"Then let's not waste another minute, Millie dear. Pack your bags.'' And with that, Millie and Lester left the kitchen and ten minutes later, the RV.

And then it was down to two.

They stood in the living room, two feet from each other. The distance seemed much further to Mark, as if the end of the competition had pushed them apart. But he knew it was more than that. Despite how far they'd come in trusting each other, Claire had kept the wall between them, refusing him an opening.

"Congratulations,'' Mark said. "You've won.''

A slow smile took over her face, reaching into her eyes and touching them with a gloss of happy tears. "I did, didn't I?''

"Well, not officially. I still have to leave.'' But Mark didn't move. His gaze drifted over Claire's face, down the soft curves of her body. He wanted nothing more than to take her in his arms and kiss her until she said yes to his proposal.

He couldn't imagine never seeing her again. Once she reached California and her father, she'd undoubtedly forget him. He was part of the past she wanted to put behind her.

The only one who would be remembering, every night of his life, would be Mark. He took a step forward, cupping her face with his hand. "Claire."

The single word was all it took to draw her into his arms, to bring her lips to his. But even as he kissed her, savoring the sweet taste of Claire, he sensed her pulling back, building that distance again.

A moment later, she broke away and took a step back. "Well, that was quite a goodbye." Her voice was shaky. "So, what are you going to do? Without the RV, how can you get the money you need for the business?"

"It doesn't matter. What matters is you being able to see your father."

"Thank you," she said quietly. "You'll never know how much that means to me."

"I think I do." He grasped her hands in his. "I meant what I said earlier about us getting married, you know."

"I know." She sighed. "I can't, Mark."

"After all we've been through, you still don't trust me?" Mark asked.

She shook her head. "It's me I don't trust. I don't know what a happy marriage looks like. Heck, I don't even know what a good relationship looks like." Her judgment of men in the past had been terrible at best. How could she know if this was the real thing? If Mark would be true to his word? If her own feelings were love and not some infatuation brought about by a week of being stuck together? She sighed. "I need more time."

The impulse to kiss her again pounded insistently in his veins. If only…

But wishes were useless. It was over. The competition. The interlude with Claire. The hope he'd had that at the last second, she'd change her mind and allow him into her heart.

"Whatever you want, Claire," he said curtly. Then he turned on his heel and headed toward the bedroom. Claire followed, taking a seat on the bed while he threw his few belongings back into the duffel.

"You were right about me," he said, forcing the levity. "I didn't bring enough."

A smile played on her lips. "Women usually are right." She turned away, toying with the television remote.

Mark hefted the bag onto his shoulder and shoved his hands into his pockets so he wouldn't touch her again. Clearly, Claire was waiting for him to leave. She didn't want him in her life beyond today. Maybe if he got off the RV fast enough, that thought wouldn't bother him so much.

"Well," he began, "to use the words of the ever-surprising Danny, I'm off." He exited the bedroom, crossed the RV in fast steps and headed for the door.

"Mark, wait."

He let go of the handle, turned to face her. "What?"

"Why are you doing this?" Claire rose and raised her hands in question. "Why are you just giving this to me?"

He took a step up, bringing them a breath apart. This time he let himself touch her. He traced along the outside of her face, memorizing. "For such a smart woman, you can be pretty dumb sometimes," he said softly. "I love you, Claire. I've loved you all my life. I just didn't realize it until now."

Her eyes widened and her jaw dropped. A heartbeat passed. Another. "You...you love me?"

"More than you know."

"Mark...I'm going to California. I can't...I can't get involved with you."

"You can't outrun your mistakes, you know. All of this," he touched her heart, "will be with you in California. And Indiana. And hell, France. I know, Claire. I tried to start over when I came back to Mercy. But it didn't work. I hadn't dealt with the past yet. Until I did, I couldn't move forward.''

''I've dealt with my past.''

''Oh yeah? Then why are you so afraid to trust me? Are you that happy being alone?''

She shook her head, looked away. ''Mark, you're asking things of me that I can't give.''

''Do you see this, Claire?'' Mark rapped on the door to the RV. ''It's a door, right?''

''Yeah.''

''You can see it as a closed door. Or you could see it as a door that could open to something else.'' In what had now become almost a natural movement for him, he reached forward and tucked an escaped tendril of her hair behind her ear. ''Close the door on your past. Open the one to your future. It's right out there, waiting for you.''

''My father. California. I can't—''

''Stop saying that and then maybe you can.'' He ran a hand through his hair and tried to temper his frustration. How he wished she'd move past this block. To see what he'd seen in the last few days. ''Let me tell you something. Until I saw you again, I might have gone right back to being the old Mark who slipped through life. But being with you has taught me I don't want to be that man anymore.'' He touched her lips with his fingertips, wanting so badly to kiss her, but knowing it would only make leaving that much harder. ''You make me want to be my best, Claire. For you. For me. For us.''

''You are the best, Mark. You're smart, you're funny, you're—''

''Not good enough for you to take a chance on, though. To really trust in love. In me.''

Claire looked away. She bit her lip and he could see the glimmer of tears in her eyes. "What if down the road it doesn't work out? What if I end up alone again?"

"And what if you don't?" Mark twisted the handle and opened the door a few inches. "Or what if you suddenly realize you love me, too? And I'm already gone."

She didn't answer him. With a heart that weighed more than the bag he carried, Mark left the RV, leaving the only woman he'd ever loved behind.

Chapter Eleven

Claire watched Mark go until he blended into the people shopping at the mall and then finally disappeared from her sight. A leaden weight settled over her.

She should be happy. She'd won. She was on her way to California. To her new life. To her father. And yet, her heart told her that by going, she was giving up something important.

She'd call her father. That would make her feel better. Claire flipped open the cell, dialed the familiar number. Her dad picked up on the second ring. Today, he sounded a bit heartier. "I'm on my way out to see you, Dad," she said. "I'm driving, so it might take a few days."

"Are you sure you want to make this move, honey? You've probably got a lot of friends in Mercy." He let out a cough, then continued. "You know, your mother always loved that town. Said it gave her a strong foundation."

"She did?"

"Yeah. We talked about getting married, settling down

there after I was done with the army. But…you know the story. Anyway, it seems to be the kind of place that grows on you. Takes root in you."

"I'm not leaving much behind, Dad." But the words scraped her throat as if they were a lie. Sharp tears stung at Claire's eyes. She swiped at them with the back of her hand. "I'll call you after I get on the road and let you know when to expect me."

"I can't wait to see you."

"Me, too." She hung up, tucking the phone into her pocket. The conversation hadn't eased the ache in her heart one bit. Had she just made a monumental mistake by turning Mark away?

A sharp knock sounded at the RV door. Claire's heart leapt into her throat. Could Mark have changed his mind? Come back to see her one last time?

Claire bounded over and flung the door open. Miss Marchand stood there, a bag from the mall's pet store in one hand and a leash in the other. At the end of the leash was a squat fuzzy retriever puppy, wagging his tail in a wild, happy frenzy.

"I suppose you still have your heart set on leaving?" Miss Marchand asked.

"Yes, I do."

The older woman heaved a sigh and pressed a hand to her bouffant. "Guess I'll have to teach that Dorene girl how to use a comb then."

Claire laughed. "If anyone can, it's you."

Miss Marchand harrumphed, but a trace of a smile edged her face. "Anyway, I'm supposed to give you this." She handed up the bag and the leash.

Claire took them and blinked in surprise. "A dog?"

"A present." Her errand completed, Miss Marchand stepped away. "If you ever come back to town, will you give an old lady a treat? Stop in and style my hair the way I like it?''

Claire smiled. ''Certainly.'' She felt a pang in her chest and reached out to grasp Miss Marchand's hand. ''I'm going to miss you and Miss Tanner.''

''Oh. You'll forget all about us.''

Claire shook her head. ''No, I don't think I will.''

''You've been like a granddaughter to me, you know,'' Miss Marchand said. ''I wish you well with your new life.''

''Thanks.'' As she clutched the hand of Miss Marchand, she realized this woman—and so many others in Mercy—had become a surrogate family to her over the years. The Doles, Jenny, The Misses. They'd cared for her, cried with her, hugged her when she needed reassurance. Cheered her accomplishments, tsk-tsked her choices in men. In short, loved her as one of their own.

Her father had been right. Mercy, and the people who comprised the family of this town, had taken root in her. Leaving it would be harder than she thought.

Miss Marchand gave Claire's hand a final squeeze. ''I'm going back to that pet shop. I saw a darling sweater for my dachshund.'' She waved, then walked away.

The puppy let out a soft bark. Claire looked down and the dog glanced back up at her, his tail starting all over again. ''Well, come on,'' she said, tugging at the leash.

The puppy charged up the stairs and into the RV, nose first. Claire dropped the bag into the chair, took a seat on the floor beside him and ruffled his ears. Attached to his collar was a note, scrawled in tight, precise handwriting. *Mark.*

Start with a puppy, Claire. And when you're ready for more, come back to me. I'm already housebroken.

Love, Mark.

The words—her words—struck Claire with monumental force. Hadn't she told him to commit to a dog first, then a woman?

Why had she been so blind? She'd missed everything. The family she already had in Mercy, the past she was running from more so than the future she was seeking. Mark had seen right through her and given her exactly what she needed. But she'd been too immersed in fear to see the love he offered.

Not the unbalanced love she'd had before, where she'd given more than she got, but a love that grew from equal give and take. From listening. And talking, sharing things she'd never shared before. From the little things, like a lock of hair tucked behind an ear, that said in so many unspoken ways that there was more than desire between them.

They'd developed a true friendship, she realized, one that served as a solid foundation for passion. A rock to build a life on. And that, Claire decided, was a good change from the headlong rush for the end zone she usually made in a relationship.

This time, she'd had more than twenty years to get to know Mark. She knew his favorite color, his weakness for chocolate mousse. And he had taken the time to know her, to pay attention.

Because he truly loved her. And if she drove away right now without taking a chance on him, she knew she'd regret it for the rest of her life.

Claire raced off the RV, the puppy clutched in her arms, nearly colliding with Nancy Lewis and the camera crew from the Lawford Ten-Spot News. A whole host of people stood behind Nancy, holding clipboards, cameras and balloons. Don Nash held a big banner that said Congratulations from Deluxe Motor Homes.

"Where are you going?" Nancy said. "You won. You can't leave now. We need to take the publicity photos."

"I have to go," Claire said. She spun around on the mall floor, looking for Mark. Surely he couldn't have gone far if he'd been at the pet store a moment ago.

"But...but you're the winner," Nancy sputtered. "You have to stay."

"Winning doesn't matter if I've lost what matters most," she said, then took off running toward the slowly retreating Miss Marchand.

The older woman just smiled when she saw Claire approach and pointed down the L-shaped hallway to the right. Claire dashed forward. The puppy let out a bark and scrambled out of her arms when Mark came into view.

He was talking to Luke, his back to her. A surge of joy rushed through her. She wasn't too late.

"Congratulations. I'm happy for you," Luke was saying.

Claire slowed her steps and pulled the puppy back. Congratulations? For what?

"Are you sure you don't want to come along?" Mark asked.

Luke shook his head. "I'm happy here, Mark. Ironically, losing the business was the best thing that ever happened. It taught me the most important thing is my daughter, my family. You did me a favor, so stop feeling guilty about it. The business was failing already and I dumped too much in your lap. When that big job fell through, there was no way for anyone to recover that company, not when the whole dot-com world was falling apart. Let it go, Mark. Move forward with what you have now. Like—"

He glanced past Mark, saw Claire and smiled. Luke tipped his head toward her, then tapped Mark's arm.

Mark wheeled around. A grin broke out on his face. The puppy lunged forward, breaking out of Claire's grasp and running toward Mark, yipping and yapping. The tile floor offered no resistance to his soft paws and he collided with Mark's feet. Mark lifted the dog into his arms and cradled him to his chest.

Claire looked at Mark and thought if getting involved with him was stupid, she might as well sign up for the lifelong learning degree. Because right now, with his sapphire eyes watching her, there seemed to be nothing smarter in the world. "Hi." She seemed to have left her vocabulary back in the RV.

"Hi yourself." He pointed toward Luke, who was walking away. "My brother came by to say my training program proposal was a hit. I owe the idea to you, you know."

"You do?"

"Yeah. When The Misses came by that day, I saw how they had a relationship with you. They knew you because you'd been their hairdresser and their friend for years. I figured if I could put that into a training program, businesses would bite."

"And they did?"

He nodded. "Luke told me they called the house and asked if I could fly out to L.A. next week to discuss implementing it." She could see the excitement and pride in his eyes.

"That's great," Claire said. "Now you'll be able to build the business up again for you and Luke."

Mark shook his head. "No, this time I'm going solo. Luke wants to stay here with Emily." Mark petted the puppy's head and the golden fuzzball snuggled closer.

She wanted to do that, too. Get close to Mark, curl against his chest and forget they were in the middle of a mall. "I think my dog likes you better."

"Give him time. Once he gets to know you, he'll fall in love. I guarantee it." In Mark's eyes, Claire saw love, felt it charge the air. Her heart raced. It wasn't too late.

"You know," she began, closing the distance between them as she talked, "I really could use a hand with that puppy. I mean, I'll be busy driving. He could eat the sofa before I noticed."

"Yeah, he would be a lot of work." Mark ruffled the pup's ears. "I hadn't thought about that when I gave him to you. Maybe I should keep him until you're ready for him?"

Claire shook her head. "I'm ready for him." She smiled. "And I'm ready for you."

He paused in petting the dog. "Are you sure?"

She nodded. "When I talked to my father today, I realized how much had been lost between him and my mother. They never got a chance together. He still loves her. I can hear it in his voice. But it's too late. She's gone." Tears threatened her eyes and her voice caught. "I don't want it to be that way for us."

"Are you saying..." Mark paused, took a breath, "you want to date me again?"

"No. I don't want that at all." She grinned when confusion flitted through his eyes. Oh, she was going to have a good time teasing him for the next fifty years of her life. "I don't want to date. I've known you for twenty years, Mark. That's a long enough courtship. You asked me to marry you earlier. Does that offer still stand?"

"Yes. Oh, yes." He put the puppy on the floor and drew Claire into his arms. "But didn't you say marriage was a huge risk?"

"You already know how I take my coffee. I'd say that's a good start." She hugged him to her. When she did, the warmth and security of Mark wrapped around her like a blanket. Home was here, she realized. Not in Mercy, or California. But with Mark. "I love you," she whispered.

He cradled her face with his hands, joy radiating in his gaze. "I've waited an awful long time to hear you say that, Claire." He smiled. "I love you, too."

"So, will you marry me?"

"Not so fast." Mark narrowed his gaze. He pulled back from her, a grin teasing at his lips. "One question first."

"What?"

"Can you make lemon meringue pie?"

She smiled. "The best."

"Okay. You have a deal. I'll marry you and make your coffee as long as you make me pie anytime I ask. And be there every day of my life."

"Done." She put out her hand. "Shall we shake on it?"

"No. I have a better idea." Mark leaned down and kissed her, taking every ounce of her soul and intensifying it. A crowd of people surrounded them. The puppy circled around them, entwining them with his leash. And somewhere in the distance, Claire could hear the frenzied cries of Nancy Lewis, still trying to get her publicity photos.

Mark ended the kiss and leaned his forehead against hers. "I think we better hit the road," he said. He hefted his bag into his hands.

"Don't you want to pack more first?" Claire asked.

He shook his head. "I have all I need right here."

"So do I," Claire said softly. "So do I."

Epilogue

"Are you ready?"

Claire smoothed her dress and adjusted her veil. "As ready as I'll ever be." She smiled down at her father, so regal in his tux, despite the wheelchair. Five months after his last treatment, his color was now full of the vibrant pink of life. Though he was still too weak to spend his day out of the wheelchair, every morning brought improvement.

The doctor had tentatively pronounced David Sawyer in remission. There were, of course, no guarantees, but that was enough of one to buy Claire the time she'd needed with her dad. They'd had a short vacation together on the RV while Mark had sewed up his training program deal in L.A. Those days with her father had brought them closer, giving Claire the familial connection she'd been seeking for so long. And now, with her and Mark living in California, she'd have many more days to share with her father. For that, Claire was grateful. In fact, today, there was an awful lot she was grateful for.

"Hey, kiddo." He took her hand. "Why are you crying?"

"Just feeling a little sentimental," she said. "And happy."

"What about nervous?"

Claire shook her head. "I don't get nervous."

Her dad laughed. "Oh yeah? Was that someone else pacing the floors of my house last night? And who spent an hour this morning calling to confirm everything she'd just confirmed yesterday?"

"Okay, maybe a little nervous," Claire admitted. "Getting married is a big step."

"The biggest. Almost as big as starting your life all over again. Not to mention enrolling in culinary school."

Those decisions hadn't seemed so big or scary, not with Mark by her side these last few months. By the summer, she'd have her degree and she could open that catering business she'd been dreaming of all her life. "With Mark, and my degree, and you…" She sighed. "I have everything I've ever wanted."

"You went after your dreams, kiddo. I admire you for that." Her father paused, gripped her hand. "You remind me so much of your mother. She had that same fire, that passion for life. She'd be so proud to see you right now."

"Oh, Dad," Claire dabbed at her eyes. "You're gonna make me cry."

He handed her his handkerchief. "You're not the only one." His voice was hoarse and in his eyes, she saw tears.

There was a knock at the door and the minister poked his head in. "It's time."

Claire nodded. She smoothed her skirt, adjusted her veil once more. She took a quick glance in the mirror, saw nothing amiss and let out her breath. "Okay. I'm ready."

The butterflies started swarming in her stomach again.

Her heart seemed to be beating in overtime, her pulse racing faster than she could even think. She moved on automatic, putting one foot in front of another, walking beside the silent roll of her father's wheelchair. They headed out of the bride's room and down the small hall to the chapel entrance.

Mark and Claire had purposely kept the wedding small, just a few friends and family members in the chapel around the corner from her father's house. No huge reception or ten-foot cake, just a small, quiet ceremony. Claire preferred it this way—the intimacy made the commitment between her and Mark seem so much more private, intense.

She took a deep breath when they reached the door leading to the chapel. An usher stepped up to pull open the heavy door.

"Wait a minute," her father said. "Not yet." He gave her hand a squeeze, then released her. Placing his palms on either arm of the chair, her father shoved himself up to a standing position. He teetered for a brief second.

Claire reached for him, but he waved her hand away and rolled the wheelchair away. "Dad! What are you doing?"

"Walking my little girl down the aisle." His smile was broad, but tears shimmered in his eyes all the same. "I'm only going to get to do this once." He put out his arm and she tucked hers into the crook. He let out a laugh. "Now *I'm* the one who's nervous."

"Don't worry," Claire said, giving his arm a squeeze, "I'll be here to hold you up." Then she took her first steps down the aisle, accompanied by the tall, distinguished man whose love had given her life. He held her tight, his hand on top of their joined arms. Tenderness swelled in her heart as the organist launched full-swing into the ''Wedding March.''

At the end of the aisle, Luke stood to the far right, her best friend Jenny on the left. Grace and John Dole, Mark's parents, were in the pews, accompanied by Matt, Katie and the twins. Emily sat behind them, flanked by Jack and Sarah and their kids. Even Nate had managed a weekend pass from the base and flown in for the event. On the bride's side sat Miss Marchand, who had pronounced a trip to California the perfect restorative for her aching joints. Claire suspected she was really there to bring all the details back to the other ladies in Flo's. Miss Tanner had come along just for company, she said, but she was wearing a new hat and brimming with pride.

And then there was Mark, who managed to look both devilish and handsome in his tux. He smiled a soft, quiet smile that seemed to exist for no one but her. ''I love you,'' he mouthed when she reached the end of the aisle.

Her father pressed a kiss to her cheek, then stepped back. Claire moved forward, taking Mark's arm now. The moment they touched, the butterflies in her stomach went away. The swell of love in her heart multiplied tenfold, nurtured by the overwhelming happiness running through her.

Thirty minutes later, Mr. and Mrs. Mark Dole dashed out of the chapel, dodging birdseed. After a flurry of kisses and good wishes, they boarded the Deluxe Motor Homes RV and started heading toward the sunset. As they pulled out of the chapel parking lot, Claire glimpsed Nancy Lewis standing on the sidewalk, flanked by a photographer. ''Just one?'' Claire asked Mark.

''Okay. Just one.'' He pulled over to the side, put the RV in Park, and then he and Claire opened the side door.

"Smile," he said to Claire when the photographer raised his camera and trained the lens on them.

"I don't think I ever stopped," she said.

Mark leaned over and whispered in her ear. "All we need now is a baby."

When the pictures of the Motor Home Marriage appeared in the *Mercy Daily News* the following day, people from all over town swore Claire Richards Dole had never looked more beautiful—or more at a total lack for words—in all her life.

* * * * *

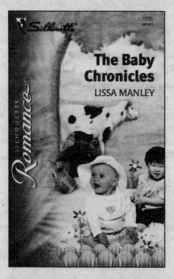

SILHOUETTE Romance®

COMING NEXT MONTH

#1702 RULES OF ENGAGEMENT—Carla Cassidy
Marrying the Boss's Daughter

Nate Leeman worked best alone, yet Wintersoft's senior VP now found himself the reluctant business partner to computer guru—and ex-girlfriend—Kat Sanderson. The hunky executive knew business and pleasure didn't mix. So why was he suddenly looking forward to long hours and late nights with his captivating co-worker?

#1703 THE BACHELOR BOSS—Julianna Morris

Sweet virgin Libby Dumont's former flame was now her boss? She'd shared one far-too-intimate kiss with the confirmed bachelor a decade ago, and although Neil O'Rourke was as handsome as ever, she knew he must remain off-limits. She just had to focus on business—*not* Neil's knee-weakening kisses!

#1704 BABY, OH BABY!—Teresa Southwick
If Wishes Were...

When Rachel Manning spoke her secret wish—to have a baby—she never expected to become an instant mother. She didn't even have a boyfriend! Yet here she was, temporary parent for a sweet month-old infant. Until Jake Fletcher— the baby's take-charge, heartbreaker-in-a-Stetson-and-jeans uncle—showed up and suggested sharing more than late-night feedings....

#1705 THE BABY CHRONICLES—Lissa Manley

Aiden Forbes was in trouble! He hadn't seen Colleen Stewart since she walked out on him eight years ago. Now he had been teamed with the marriage-shy journalist to photograph an article on babies, and seeing Colleen surrounded by all these adorable infants was giving Aiden ideas about a baby of their own!

SRCNM1203